PRAISE FOR *WHERE WE GO FROM HERE*

'A remarkably honest story about love, lust and HIV in today's world' David Levithan

'A powerfully honest book. Its raw and beautiful emotions will bring you to tears and leave you shouting with joy' Rachael Lippincott

'Captivating . . . a story of friendship, love and self-acceptance' Jonathan Van Ness

'This treatise on community provides comfort in an often homophobic world . . . simply fearless' *Kirkus* starred review

'The story is universal . . . it fills an urgent need . . . this deserves the widest possible readership' *Booklist* starred review

'Effectively explores the tensions that stem from the prejudice and fear surrounding HIV' *Publishers Weekly*

'An authentic, deeply felt debut . . . chock-full of poignant conversation starters' *School Library Journal*

'Tackles the taboo subject of prejudice against those who are HIV positive with joy and humanity' 2021 GLLI *Translated YA Book Prize* (co-winner)

'A deeply heartwarming story about friendship, found family, and the journey to overcoming your fears' *The Nerd Daily*

'Rocha lets his characters make mistakes, learn, fight, grow, change, al,

# WHERE
# WE
# GO
# FROM
# HERE

## LUCAS ROCHA

TRANSLATED BY LARISSA HELENA

**David Fickling Books**
31 Beaumont Street
Oxford OX1 2NP, UK

Where We Go From Here
is a
DAVID FICKLING BOOK

Originally published in Brazilian Portuguese in 2018 as Você Tem a Vida Inteira
by Galera Record

First published in Great Britain in 2021 by
David Fickling Books,
31 Beaumont Street,
Oxford, OX1 2NP

www.davidficklingbooks.com

Hardback edition published 2021
This edition published 2022

978-1-78845-192-5

1 3 5 7 9 10 8 6 4 2

Papers used by David Fickling Books are from well-managed forests and other
responsible sources.

DAVID FICKLING BOOKS Reg. No. 8340307

A CIP catalogue record for this book is available from the British Library.

Printed and bound in Great Britain by Clays Ltd, Elcograf S.p.A.

FOR EVERYONE WHO LIVES WITH HIV,
DIRECTLY OR INDIRECTLY

# CHAPTER 1

# IAN

THE FIRST STEP IS ADMITTING to yourself that, no matter the outcome, life goes on.

The clinic is packed with people walking in every direction: To the left, a child is running in circles while an exhausted mother tries to calm her down. To the side, a man in his seventies rocks back and forth on a cane, refusing every courteous offer of a seat. A little farther down, the door to one of the exam rooms is ajar and a doctor is scanning a medical chart for information while a woman sitting across from her waits anxiously. To my right, a tall guy with a blue streak in his hair is staring at his phone, his foot tapping as nervously as mine, and I can tell that even though he's looking at the device, he's not paying the slightest bit of attention to it.

And in the middle of all this hubbub, of doctors and nurses walking this way and that, of people dissatisfied with the long wait time for appointments and a dusty fan that makes more noise than ventilation, I wait.

"Ian Gonçalves?"

A woman with shoulder-length blond hair and the coldest blue eyes I've ever seen looks at me; a folded piece of paper rests in her hand as she closes the door to the lab behind her. She has wrinkles that she's probably tried to cover up with Botox injections and the full lips of someone who's tried rejuvenating fillers, and there's a gold necklace with a heart-shaped pendant hanging from her neck.

I press my finger against a cotton ball that absorbs a drop of blood (I had to come back in for a second rapid HIV test because they told me my blood clotted the first time and they needed another sample) and ask myself if those cold blue eyes bring good news or bad.

I nod, and she signals for me to stand up.

"This way, please." She turns her back to me and walks to a door at the end of the hallway. She doesn't even look to check if I'm following her. Maybe she's just used to the veiled nervousness that comes with getting tested for HIV.

The blue-haired guy next to me waves and parts his lips into a supportive smile, as if wishing me luck. His finger is also pressed against a cotton ball as he waits for his own results.

I go down the hallway, and it morphs into a blur; I'm dizzy with anxiety, sweaty from the heat, and exhausted from all the waiting. It's been only thirty minutes but feels like an eternity.

The therapist's office, just like the rest of the clinic, isn't in the best shape: There's a bucket behind her desk, where drops from a leak fall sporadically and monotonously. The desk is made of wood, and the sawdust on the ground points to a termite infestation. The fan spins lazily overhead, spreading dust and making the October heat even more unbearable in this tiny room with nothing but a jammed window to let some air in.

"Please have a seat."

My impression of this woman is that it's impossible to like her right away. She has a sour taste about her, as if it's her job to give bad news on a daily basis and she isn't exactly comfortable with it.

"Why did you decide to get tested, Ian?"

Good question. I could tell her the truth about my sex life, about the two times I threw caution to the wind and didn't use a condom because I thought it would be a one-time thing; or I could lie and say that I got a tattoo from a hippie, and the needle he used was rustier than a piece of iron cast out to sea. Whatever my answer, the last thing I want is to face her judgment.

"I found out you provide rapid HIV testing here. I'm eighteen, and I've never gotten tested before, so I decided I should," I say, half-lying, half-truthful, looking into those ice-cold eyes that won't stop analyzing me.

The truth is, I have no idea why the hell I chose to come here. The only reason I'm not 100 percent regretting being here and having to look this woman in the face is that my health is more important than anything else. Do I *need* a reason to know my status? Every ad I see about this topic says it's important to know your status regardless of your lifestyle or what you do in your free time. And the first thing the therapist asks me is *Why did you decide to get tested?*

Honestly, if the idea here is not to play the blame game, then her technique needs a lot of work.

"Hmm . . ." she mumbles, looking at the folded paper in front of her. She hands me my ID, and I put it back in my wallet.

Silence fills every corner of the room for a couple of seconds, but in my mind it feels like a whole week has gone by.

"I'm afraid I don't have good news." She unfolds the paper, and that's indication enough that, yeah, my life is about to change forever.

The paper is marked up in blue ink, and there's an X between two parentheses next to three uppercase letters:

(x) HIV+

( ) Syphilis

( ) Hepatitis C

"The good news is that the results came back negative for syphilis and hepatitis C." She tries to smile, and I do the same in the face of what she's calling good news. "The bad . . ." She doesn't finish the sentence but points to the other markings on the paper, showing that the results for the two different blood samples (so that's why they asked for another sample!) are both positive.

I remain silent, and she hands me the paper.

What does she expect me to do? Frame it?

"Do you know who might have infected you?"

Infected. As if I were an addict's fucking syringe.

"No" is my answer.

Because it's the truth, but it's also a lie. I know who it *could* have been, but there's only a 50 percent chance that I'm right. And it's not like I'm still in touch with either of those guys, or like I can remember their names or know how to find them.

But, hey, this isn't supposed to be about blame, right?

"Really?" she insists. "It's important that you have a conversation with whomever might—"

"No," I repeat firmly.

"All right. Are you in a relationship?"

"No."

"Have you had sexual intercourse without a condom in the last few months?"

"No."

"Not even oral sex?"

I remain silent, staring at the floor, tired of this interrogation.

"Ian, it's important that you speak with your past partners so that they can get tested, too." Her voice is almost kind now, as if she's suddenly realized that she's dealing with a human being and not a goddamn wall. "The sooner you tell them, the sooner they can make arrangements to get tested. Understand?"

"Mhm."

More silence.

"Where do we go from here?" I ask.

*We.* I try using the plural pronoun so I can feel a little more supported, but in this moment I know I am all alone.

"You will be directed to the infectious diseases department, where you'll do another round of exams to confirm the rapid test. After that, it's typical to start treatment right away." She opens a drawer gnawed by termites and hands me a photocopy. "Bring a copy of these documents to the reception desk so we can put all the bureaucracy behind us."

The woman sighs, tired, showing a sign of humanity for only the second time this afternoon.

My ears are buzzing; I feel numb and certain that if I take a deeper breath, I'll start crying. So I focus and stare at the leak in the ceiling.

"Look," she continues. "People don't have to die from this anymore. If you follow proper treatment, your life can be as normal as anyone else's. But I'll let the infectious diseases specialist discuss all that with you."

*You*, she said.

In the singular.

I'm completely alone.

I look at the list of documents: ID, proof of residence, social security card, and public health insurance card, which I have no idea how to get.

"How are you feeling?" she asks.

I try to spot a hint of compassion in her voice, but it's an automatic question, simply protocol.

"We have to keep moving forward, right?" I smile, loudly repeating the plural *we*, reaffirming that I am not alone, and telling myself that I can't start crying in front of her. "I hope it all works out."

"It will," she says encouragingly, smiling for the first time since she first laid her blue eyes on me. "If you need any support, you can go to our psychology department, or to social services. Here at the health center, you'll get everything you need. And one of the great advantages is that here in Brazil, the public health system covers the entire treatment without much of a hassle, all of it for free. You're in good hands."

*You, you, you.*

She never fails to emphasize the singular.

I am all alone.

# CHAPTER 2

# VICTOR

THE GUY WHO WAS AHEAD of me at the clinic leaves the therapist's office, holding a folded piece of paper, his head down. His eyes aren't swollen, and I didn't hear any shouting while he was in there, but he walks by quickly without looking at anyone.

I'm sure the diagnosis wasn't good. If it were, he'd be smiling from ear to ear.

The therapist walks out right after him and goes into the lab again, where she picks up another folded piece of paper and an ID.

"Victor Mendonça?" She seems tired when I get up and nod. Her eyes are pretty, a deep blue like the sky of an autumn afternoon. "Shall we?"

I follow her to the end of the hallway, the tips of my fingers aching. My nails are all but gone from my nervous nail biting, and I'm certain I'll cry like a baby if the results come back positive.

Why did Henrique do this to me? Why did he wait until *after* we'd had sex to tell me that he was positive?

"Please have a seat." She points to a wobbly chair with yellow foam peeking out of two rips in the corners, and I comply, feeling my legs tremble and my stomach churn.

When I seem at least minimally comfortable, she hands me the ID and asks, "Why did you decide to get tested, Victor?"

I consider it for a few seconds before I speak.

"I met a guy, Henrique, and he has always been a sweetheart to me. We started going out, and things got pretty intense between us. We talked all the time, went to the movies, made out, and all that. And then we had sex." Before I realize it, the words tumble out of my mouth. "The next day—that is, two days ago—he sent me a text saying he was positive and asking if I still wanted to go out with him, the bastard! Then I got paranoid and searched for the closest testing center, and I found you."

"Did you use protection?"

"Yes, of course, even for oral sex. He said it was absolutely necessary, and I even thought he was making a fuss, because, like, who uses a condom for oral sex, you know? And then everything started to make sense. I don't know, at first I thought he was just being super cautious, not that he was sick. His text said he was something called 'undetectable,' I guess, so I looked it up. From what I can tell, it means he's on medication and can't transmit the virus. But I could still have caught it from him, right? Like, he had an *obligation* to tell me he was sick before I got into bed with him."

"He had the *option* to tell you that he's positive, Victor," she corrects me, and the authority in her voice makes me want to swallow some of what I just said. "And he's not sick; he simply has the virus in his system. His only obligation is to use protection, and he did. Most people I know who test positive say it's not very easy to open up about this subject with others."

I sit with her words in silence, unable to rebut them.

A while later, the therapist asks, "Was this guy the only one you've had sexual intercourse with recently? Did you have sex with another partner, with or without protection?"

What does this lady take me for? A *slut*?

"No," I mutter in response, maybe a little offended by the question or the fact that she said Henrique didn't have an obligation to tell me anything. Of course he did.

Then I feel my stomach turn to ice, because she still hasn't unfolded the paper and she's building all this suspense just to give me my results.

"Ma'am, can we just cut to the chase?"

She must find something funny, because she smiles before unfolding the paper and handing it to me.

( ) HIV+

( ) Syphilis

( ) Hepatitis C

"The tests came back negative," she says.

I let out a sigh of relief. "So that's it? Everything's okay with me?"

"Yes. This partner of yours appears to have been very responsible for insisting on using a condom and, I have to admit, seems like a great guy for opening up to you about his status, even though he had no obligation to do so. Doesn't seem like the kind of guy you just throw away."

"He could have infected me!"

"The chances of transmission by someone who doesn't know whether they're infected are much higher than by those who are on treatment, and *especially* if they are undetectable—which it sounds like he is, meaning he can't transmit the virus," she explains, interlacing her fingers, and I notice a hint of impatience in her voice. "Well, I think we're done here. I'm happy everything is fine with you, Victor, and I hope you and . . . Henrique, is it? I hope you two sort it out. In the meantime, you can go home."

I feel the weight of the world lift from my shoulders when she hands me the paper without any Xs on it. Everything seems more colorful now, and all the apprehension I've felt the last couple of days seems to have disappeared in the blink of an eye.

"The other guy who was in here before me . . . did he test positive?" I ask, trying to start a conversation as I get up. "He didn't look too happy."

"I can't discuss another patient's test results," she says, standing from her chair to open the door of the mildewy room. "Patient confidentiality."

Looks like I won't extract anything else from her. So I just nod, shove the piece of paper and ID in my pocket, and leave. All I know is that I never want to set foot in a testing center or hear another word about HIV again.

+

"Sandra?" The first person I call when I get to the bus station is my best friend. She's probably waiting for a text (because while I was in the waiting room, we exchanged a million messages in which she tried to reassure me and I was in a state of despair). "It came back negative! Everything is fine!"

"I told you that you were being paranoid, Victor!" she answers on her end, but I notice that her voice sounds as relieved as mine. "I only met Henrique once, but he seems like a nice guy. I mean, he was super honest. You could give him a chance."

*He has a disease that can kill me*, I think of saying. *I don't want anything to do with him anymore!*

No, that would be too cruel and would get Sandra started on one of her politically correct rants about how we should embrace all differences. So I take the diplomatic approach.

"He could have been honest *before* we had sex," I reply, looking over my shoulder to make sure no one is eavesdropping.

"And you could be less dramatic. It's not as if he refused to use a condom. From what you told me, *you* were the one who wasn't really into the idea of using a condom for oral."

I still can't bring myself to accept that Henrique was right to hide this from me, but it seems like my silence is all Sandra wants to hear. So I change the subject.

"Why don't we meet up? You know, to celebrate?" I ask.

"It's Tuesday, Victor. We have class in the morning. How about over the weekend?"

"Deal. But if you flake, I'll never speak to you again."

Maybe she's right about my penchant for drama, but hell if I'll concede that I agree with her. Deep down, she already knows, anyway.

"If you say so" is all she says before hanging up.

I shove the phone into my pocket, smiling.

"Congrats." A voice catches me by surprise.

I was so relieved by the good news that I didn't even notice someone had sat down next to me at the bus stop—the same guy who'd left the therapist's office before I walked in.

He's still holding the folded piece of paper. His hair is shaved short, and he has a thick, well-trimmed beard over his tanned face. His eyes are two big, brown, reddened orbs, but I see no sign of tears. He has the build of someone who hits the gym every now and again, with wide shoulders and biceps popping out of the sleeves of his shirt. His jeans squeeze his legs, maybe a full two sizes too small for his thick thighs.

"Sorry, I didn't mean . . ." I let the words die on my lips as my ears start to burn. I know I shouldn't feel guilty for being happy about my negative test result, but I feel horrible for making him listen as I celebrated it.

"It's okay," he answers with a melancholy smile.

"Bad news?"

He nods in resignation.

I'm not sure what makes me do it, but I sit by his side, the hot wind making my ears burn even harder, and I start talking.

"You know it's not a death sentence anymore, right?" I know I'm being such a hypocrite, but the words come out automatically. "I did some research before getting tested and read all kinds of stories about people with HIV who lead normal lives. Everything is going to be all right."

He's still looking down, unable to lift his gaze. I want to say he should hold his head up high and face the world, but I don't know how I would have reacted if the news hadn't been good for me. I'd probably be locked in the bathroom of that clinic, crying inside a stall and thinking the world was unfair as hell and that I didn't deserve this.

"I just . . . thought the results would be different," he says, still looking down, his voice hoarse. He clears his throat, takes a deep breath, and bites his lip. "We never think everything will go wrong until it does, right?"

And with that, he breaks down.

He presses the palms of his hands against his face and lets the paper with his diagnosis fall to the ground. I get up and grab the sheet of paper before the wind carries it away. His back arches up and down as he sobs, completely out of control, and all I want is to give him a hug—this guy I don't even know—and tell him that, yeah, it will be hard, but things can still work out.

But who am I to say that? What gives me the authority? Me, who five minutes ago thought HIV was the worst thing that could ever happen to a person?

So I don't say anything. I just stay by his side and put a hand on his shoulder, trying to comfort him as best I can.

He continues to sob, and on an impulse, I wrap him in a hug as he buries his face in my arm. I feel his hot tears soaking the sleeve of my shirt, but I don't mind. All I want right now is for him to feel better, and I know that a hug is much more powerful than any word I can say in a moment like this.

My eyes water when he finally calms down. I want to cry, too, even though I don't have the slightest idea who this guy is or what happened to him to make him end up at this clinic, testing positive for HIV. But I take a deep breath and play the strong character I never am in any other situation.

"I'm sorry, this is so . . . ridiculous," he says, half laughing and half crying, pushing away from me and wiping his tears on the backs of his hands. "You don't even know me, and . . . I'm sorry."

"No need to apologize." I try a half smile but fail. "What are you going to do now?"

He takes a deep breath before answering.

"Probably lock myself in my room and listen to Lana Del Rey until morning."

I can't help but laugh at his sarcastic remark.

"If you want to really wallow in self-pity, I recommend Johnny Hooker."

"Never heard of him."

"He's really good. If you really want to wallow in self-pity, I mean. Here . . ." Another one of my impulsive actions: I don't really know what makes me grab a pen from my pocket and the paper with his test results, but when I catch myself, I'm already nervously, shakily scribbling my name and phone number on the back of the sheet. I hand it to him. "If you need to talk to someone, you can text me. A friend of mine is also positive, and I can put the two of you in touch."

Henrique appears in my mind's eye, and though I wouldn't want to see him even if he were the last man on earth, I don't think he'd be opposed to talking to someone who is about to go through all the same struggles he must have faced when he was first diagnosed.

"Thank you"—he looks at the scrawl on the paper—"Victor. And I'm sorry for all this."

"No worries, um . . ." I answer with a smile.

"Ian. My name is Ian."

"No need to apologize, Ian." I look up and see my bus coming down the street. "Are you going to be okay?"

"Yeah."

I stand up and hail the bus. I get on, swipe my card to release the turnstile, and, before we pull away, look back at the bus stop.

Ian smiles and waves, and then he's out of sight.

Even though I don't know him, and I'm pretty sure I'll never see him again, I hope he will be all right.

# CHAPTER 3

# HENRIQUE

VICTOR STILL HASN'T REPLIED TO my last text. I wonder what he's thinking.

I look at the long message I sent him, with the little Read under the balloon confirming that he's already seen it.

Henrique:

I'm not quite sure if it's fair to tell you this over text, but I think you need to know, especially because I'm really into you, and the last thing I want is to start whatever this is with a lie or, as I see it, an omission of the truth. No need to worry—for real— but I'm HIV-positive. I take good care of myself and take all my meds, so I'm undetectable. And since we used a condom, there's no problem. If you still want to talk to me, I'll wait for your reply. I'm sorry for not telling you sooner. I usually don't, and it's

> always hard to talk about this with anybody, mostly
> because I haven't had great experiences in the past.
> So, there it is. Get back to me when you have a
> chance.

I lock my phone with a sigh, looking over the mess of the apartment I share with my roommate, Eric. There are sequined clothes and makeup scattered on every possible surface, and three wigs balance precariously on the backs of our dining room chairs.

This has happened before, but it always hurts when the texts that seemed so intimate and full of excitement simply stop coming. Some people say HIV is the love virus, because it becomes this insurmountable barrier to the things that might happen if it weren't there. And even though HIV has been my unwanted partner for three years, like an intrusive brother-in-law who takes over the guest room, it's still hard to deal with all the impossibilities that it imposes on my life.

"You're not checking your messages again, are you, you whore?" Eric looks over my shoulder, eyeing my phone. His attention is split between his own cell phone and a YouTube video on his laptop, in which an Argentinian drag queen gives a tutorial on how to do Elizabeth Taylor's makeup from *Cleopatra*. Eric is preparing for his next show, and the theme of the party is ancient Egypt. "If you would just quit all the apps and start looking for people in real life, I'm sure you wouldn't get so frustrated."

"Says the saint who has a profile on every dating app known to man," I respond, knowing that Eric is a fixture on all the hookup apps, whether they're meant for gay, straight, bi, or trans people.

He's even on a few for lesbians. (Seriously, he claims it's so he can make friends.) "I think I fucked it all up again."

I open my messages and show him the text I sent Victor. He pauses the YouTube video and grabs my phone to read it.

Eric is, so far, the only person who knows I'm positive and still replies to my texts. We've known each other since we were fifteen, and in all that time, he hasn't changed much: over six feet tall, dark brown skin, and thin arms. The only things that have changed are his teeth, now perfectly straight thanks to the braces and incredibly white after bleaching; his hair, which he used to shave but now wears full and always in a different stylish hairdo; and his complexion, now soft and blemish-free after a dermatological treatment that nearly left him bankrupt.

As for me, I'm basically the same as when we were teenagers, too. Five foot eight (the famous puberty growth spurt passed me by, and I went from being the tallest among my friends to being the shortest in less than two years), with rust-colored hair and white skin, as if I were allergic to the sun. My teeth are crooked, my muscles are still under the regular promise that I'll start working out before I give up on going to the gym for the twentieth time, and my wrists are always hurting from the hours of photoshopping at the advertising agency where I work.

Eric was and continues to be a part of my life, through all the ups and downs—from the fits of laughter to the sleepless nights on the phone, hearing me cry and complain about how unfair life is and how useless everything can be, since in the end we're all going to die anyway.

And, as a result of our friendship and the trust I placed in him, I decided to share an apartment with him when things got complicated for him at home, even if he can be a chaotic hurricane of glitter and multicolored fabrics. I consider him my Jiminy Cricket, my Voice of Reason, or whatever it is that people call their conscience, especially because he's the only one who doesn't just smile and nod at whatever nonsense the antiretrovirals evoke when they insist on messing with my emotions.

"Henrique, you know that you have to be patient, especially with the younger boys." He opens Victor's picture on my phone, staring at his pale, smiling face; his light hair—full in the middle and shaved on the sides, with a blue streak right up front; and his green eyes that are almost indistinguishable behind the reflection in his vintage glasses that are too big for his face. Then Eric gives me my phone and returns to his own. "How old is this boy?"

"Eighteen."

"And you're twenty-one. It may not seem like it, but that's a big difference. He's probably scared, and you know very well that it's a rational reaction. At least he didn't make up a story about his grandmother in New Zealand needing surgery to remove a tumor or some shit like that other guy did."

He's talking about Carlos, the first and only asshole who managed to break my heart, not to mention leave me forever hesitant to open up to anyone who crosses my path. And as a bonus, he also made me hate New Zealand.

"I hate New Zealand," I whisper.

"Just because your ex went there to pretend like you don't exist?"

"He went there because he is a coward who's afraid to be the person he really is. I hate New Zealand, *The Lord of the Rings*, and that Vegemite crap they eat."

"Sweetie, you've never even tried it."

"It smells like boiled beer and looks like tar. There's no way it's good."

"Okay, and you hate New Zealand because one of the biggest series in film history was shot there. And that's important because . . . ?"

"It's not important! Jesus, Eric, six years of friendship and you still haven't realized that I dislike things for totally irrational reasons? You should be used to it by now."

"All right, let's not talk about the hobbits of New Zealand. Or horrible ex-boyfriends. Have you tried calling this guy?" Eric asks, referring to the message I sent Victor.

"He saw the message but never replied. That's the twenty-first-century version of not picking up the phone."

"You can try to call and have a conversation. Like, you had sex *after* you learned his name and went on, like, five bad dates in two weeks. You're practically married in this day and age."

"And *I'm* the app queen," I say, giving him a dirty look. He's still looking at his phone, and in the reflection on his glasses, I can see the yellow glow of Grindr.

"What?" He looks at me and closes the app. "Don't even; I'm not the one who's in love here."

"I'm not in love."

"Okay, so you just 'care too much,'" he says, making air quotes as he balances his phone in his right hand.

"Don't do that."

"What?"

"'This,'" I answer, imitating his hand gesture. "It's ridiculous."

"'Ridiculous'?" He does it again.

I roll my eyes and ignore him, looking down at my phone.

The ellipsis bubble pops up on my screen, indicating that Victor is typing a response.

My heart starts racing.

"I think he's about to send something."

Eric locks his phone and peeks over my shoulder.

"It's not a dick pic, is it?"

"Shut up, Eric."

We wait for the message, and it comes in short sentences. As I read, I'm both relieved and confused by it.

Victor:

Hi

I got tested

It came back negative

And I met a guy there

His came back positive

I don't know why, but I thought of you

I said if he needed to talk to someone

> He could talk to you
>
> Still a little confused by all of this
>
> But idk
>
> The guy didn't seem too good
>
> If he messages me, can I give him your number?
>
> His name is Ian

I stare at the screen, processing the information.

"Aw, how cute, he thought of you! At least this one didn't run away to New Zealand for years and pretend you never existed." Eric smiles. "What are you going to say?"

"That I don't want my status to be on the evening news," I answer, but before I can say more, Eric rips the phone out of my hand and starts typing.

> Henrique:
>
> Sure.
>
> If you want to talk about us, I'm here.
>
> I'm glad the test came back negative.

At this stage of the game, Eric's meddling in my personal life isn't a nuisance anymore. And honestly, I even like it when he plays Cupid and replies to messages on my behalf, because most of the time I say it's not worth pursuing something that won't work out in the end. He says that's just my negativity speaking and that if I at least put in some effort, things could be different.

"He knows about the window period, right?" Eric asks. He has learned so much about HIV from me, either from my endless conversations on the subject or from his research during the first months of my diagnosis, when he tried to show me through graphs, charts, and stats that I was not going to die anytime soon.

"Probably not, but he could have researched it. And I already said I took all necessary precautions, as I always do. And that I'm undetectable, which means—"

"The chance of transmitting the virus is effectively zero," Eric says automatically, a bored tone in his voice. He's heard me talk about it at least two hundred times. "Now you want to preach to the choir?"

"I think there's nothing else I can teach you that you don't already know, young Padawan," I say. Eric ignores my comment and presses play on his makeup tutorial.

I stare at Victor's message, wondering if he's worth the trouble or if I should let him go.

He did respond, even if he didn't talk directly about the two of us, and that's already more than most guys do. Most of them believe that silence is the best medicine, but in reality, it messes with my emotions more than any antiretroviral ever could.

# CHAPTER 4

# IAN

WHEN I GET HOME, I'M met with pure silence. There are papers strewn about the dining room table—engineering blueprints my mom brings home from work—and a coffee-stained mug that for some reason she didn't put in the sink. A photo of the whole family (me, my mom and dad, and my younger sister) sits atop a small table near the TV; it's the only picture we posed for during our trip to João Pessoa. There's a note from Mom underneath the frame that says she and Dad will be home late and asks me to make dinner for myself and my sister, who's still at school.

Crying in front of that stranger was embarrassing, but at least it seems to have removed something bad from my system. I let out an exhausted breath, throw my backpack on a chair, open the fridge, and swig a drink of water straight from the bottle. I open the vegetable drawer and take out some broccoli, an eggplant, and an onion. From the shelf above it, I grab a package of unseasoned chicken cutlets. I open the pantry, pull out a bag of brown rice, and start boiling some water. I do it all automatically and wonder if that old saying—that food made with love tastes better—is true. If so, this dinner won't be a very good one.

I don't want to think about HIV, but the three letters dance relentlessly in front of me, reminding me there's something inside my body that shouldn't be there and that, little by little, is destroying me. It's hard not to think about death when it's running through your veins.

I cut the eggplant into thin slices and the broccoli into small florets, and when I start dicing the onion, the knife slips in my hand and digs into my fingertip, letting a small trickle of blood stain the vegetable red.

One look at the wound, and my stomach churns. Ignoring the burning sensation running up my hand, I drop the knife and grab a paper towel, pressing it against my finger as I watch my blood dissolve into the white layers of the half-chopped onion.

I pull a chair behind me and sit down, and my eyes start stinging—not because of the onion but from sadness.

Is this what my life is going to be like from now on? Taking care not to shed even a single drop of blood so others will never come into contact with this virus that lives inside me, killing me bit by bit? Is this what I am now, a walking HIV container, about to infect anyone who comes near me?

The tears running down my face are born of anger and frustration, because I know I can no longer ignore the fact that I've hurt myself. I can't just go back in time to redo those nights when I didn't use condoms and slept with guys I didn't even know, whom I will never see again.

I'm disgusted by myself. Disgusted by my memories and the things I've done to get to this point. They say that when you're diagnosed with HIV, it's not supposed to be about guilt or blame or fault, but that's all I feel right now. Guilt for being stupid, for allowing myself to get caught up in the heat of the moment, for having to carry inside me this thing that no one can remove.

I wait for my finger to stop bleeding, then throw the onion in the trash. I snatch the knife that cut me and toss it in the boiling water that was going to cook the rice, all the while knowing it's irrational. I want to sterilize the knife, the onion, the cutting board—my own body. I want to drink this pot of boiling water so it can burn away the virus inside me, but I know that's impossible.

It's pointless to cry, but I can't stop.

It's useless to rehash these thoughts, but that's all I can do.

It's hopeless to think that my life won't be different, because that's exactly what it will be.

I wish it didn't have to.

+

The following days are a mess, especially because I need to make excuses to justify my coming and going at unusual hours.

The dynamics at home are a little different from traditional families: Adriana, my mom, works extremely odd hours and has meetings left and right all over Rio de Janeiro and sleepless nights during which she draws, calculates, and revises plans for civil engineering briefs. Right now she's working on three different blueprints, and the dark circles under her eyes are proof that she is way too tired. William, my dad, is more resistant to sleep deprivation and sleeps between four and five hours a night. He teaches math at three different schools in addition to being a math tutor on weekends to help make ends meet, which just barely affords us the overpriced luxury of living near the subway in Rio's Botafogo district, in a tiny two-bedroom apartment. Vanessa, my sister, goes to school in the mornings and to a college prep course in the afternoons, and when she's not out, she buries her face in her biology textbooks, committed to her dream of getting into medical school.

"Do you have class today?" my mom asks when she sees me at seven a.m., filling my backpack with things I won't actually be using that day. It's Thursday, and I don't have class on Thursdays.

"I need to drop by school to finish a microeconomics assignment," I whisper, stuffing the documents that need to be photocopied into a folder and tucking it into my backpack, along with my HIV test result that has Bus Stop Guy's number scribbled on it and a book that I hope will help distract me in the waiting room.

"Okay," she says, lost in her own calculations. I realize she's still wearing yesterday's clothes.

"Mom, did you get any sleep?"

"Sleep is for the weak." She grabs her coffee mug and extends it toward me as if she's toasting, then brings it to her mouth and takes a long gulp. "These plans had to be done two days ago."

"You're going to make yourself sick."

She smiles and looks at me, noticing my expression. "Is everything okay, Ian?"

I try to disguise my dismay. "Why wouldn't it be?"

"You look awful. Did you spend the whole night bingeing Netflix again?"

The good news is that she gave me a pretty solid excuse herself.

"Yeah. There were just six episodes left in the season."

"*Just* six episodes? Honestly, I would love to know where you find the patience." She turns her attention back to the blueprints spread on the table. "I hope you get some sleep tonight for a change. Sleep is important, you know."

"Sleep is for the weak," I answer with a smile, opening the front door and walking to the elevator.

I wonder if it would be a good idea to tell my mom about my diagnosis. I mean, we have a healthy relationship, even if we're not exactly confidants. She's much easier to talk to than my dad, for instance, who hasn't really accepted the fact that I'm gay and prefers to believe it's just a matter of time until I get a girlfriend and that one of these days I'll show up on the doorstep with the mother of his grandchildren.

I couldn't sleep last night. I spent way too much time crying into my pillow, careful not to make any noise and wake Vanessa—which would have been hard, since she sleeps so heavily that not even her alarm clock on the loudest setting can wake her up in the morning.

When I finally stopped crying, I lay in bed wide-awake, letting the bad thoughts overcome me. What will the HIV take away from me? Will I be capable of being the same person I've always been, of taking risks, of falling in love, having a family, traveling, sky-diving, studying abroad, drinking—of being happy? Or will my entire life be defined by this virus? Will this gray cloud that seems to overshadow everything last forever? Will I ever again be able to think that things can turn out all right and that life is worth living?

At the same time, I thought about Gabriel, my best friend. I still haven't told him about my diagnosis. In fact, I haven't told anybody about it except that guy at the bus stop. It's not as if I have a lot of friends at school with whom I could have a conversation like this. People say I'm a little averse to friendship, and that might be true. I haven't even replied to Gabriel's last message—a simple "What's up?"—as if, bizarrely, he already knew that things weren't going well and that I needed someone to talk to.

I don't know if I want to go through the process of calling him, telling him the truth, and enduring the silence from the other side, even if, somehow, I know that he'll support me. I don't want him to look at me differently, or to judge me, or to say anything that could hurt me even more, because I simply can't handle that right now. But if I'm wrong, and he doesn't support me, what can I expect from others?

When the sun came in through my bedroom curtains, the only conclusion I could come to was that I needed to get up and set things in order.

+

The nurse's office is cold from the powerful air conditioner, and it doesn't look anything like the shabby and claustrophobic office of the therapist who saw me two days ago. This place is airy and sterile, with a cabinet full of medicine locked behind glass, a bed covered in a hospital sheet, a scale, and a small table where a nurse is sitting.

Somehow, she makes me feel calmer. Maybe it's her perfect smile or her neat hairdo, with not one single strand out of place. It may be the fact that she's not even thirty, or it might be her immaculately white scrubs. Perhaps it's her posture, both professional and welcoming, or even the simple fact that she does not seem inclined to treat me like I'm terminally ill.

"Did you bring copies of your documents?" she asks, and I hand them to her. Her skin is black, and her eyes are round and brown, watching as if trying to decipher me before I say a word.

The nurse unfolds the papers, checks to make sure everything is in order, and retrieves a piece of lined paper from a folder. She glues a passport photo in a square that's meant to serve that specific purpose and jots down some basic information from my ID, and in the meantime, I remain silent. Her handwriting is curvy and careful, very different from the chicken scratch that doctors scrawl on their prescription pads.

When she's done filling everything out, she looks up at me and smiles.

I smile back mechanically.

"So, Iago . . . before we start, I want you to know that this facility offers everything you need to ensure you receive proper treatment."

"Ian," I say under my breath.

"Sorry?"

"You called me Iago. My name is Ian."

"Oh, of course!" Her smile widens pleasantly, and she seems a little embarrassed by her mistake. "I'm sorry about that. But you look like an Iago, you know? Has anyone ever told you that?"

"Actually, no."

"Well, okay, Ian." She offers her hand, and I shake it. "My name is Fernanda. How are you?"

"I'm okay . . ."

"Hard for someone to feel okay after receiving the kind of news you got. How are you *really*?"

"Scared," I answer, trying to sum up all my feelings in one word. Maybe this is the only word that comes close to the real feeling.

"And that's understandable. Here's what I can tell you: From now on, you'll need to take a few extra precautions and have some different routines from what you're used to. But it's no mystery. Brazil has one of the most effective HIV treatment programs in the world."

I look at the medicine cabinet and notice a bunch of different containers with strange names.

"Are all of these part of the treatment?"

"Yes, but you won't have to take all of them," she answers. "Treatment for HIV has evolved a lot over the years, and all these medicines you see here are different options. What you need to understand, Iago, is that every body is different, and the virus manifests differently in each one; that's why we have so many options. But most patients we treat use that one over there." She points to a container that looks like a vitamin bottle. "We call it the three-in-one, which means it has three antiretroviral drugs in one single pill."

I ignore the fact that she just got my name wrong again.

"One pill?" I ask. Whenever I've heard the expression *cocktail therapy* for HIV, I thought it would be at least a dozen pills at once.

"One pill, once a day, and that's the end of it. That's the basic, most common treatment, unless you experience any unexpected side effects. But that's a conversation you'll have with the doctor at Infectious Diseases when you get to meet her. The treatment is simple and very effective, and even though we're still not very close to a proper cure, strictly speaking, it is still possible to lead a relatively normal daily life. If you follow the treatment, your life expectancy will be identical to that of someone who is HIV-negative. And I'll also point out, Iago, that people living with HIV who take their medication consistently cannot transmit the virus to others."

"Ian."

"Sorry?"

"You called me Iago again. It's Ian."

"Oh my God!" She laughs and shakes her head, and I think it's funny because I know she's not doing it on purpose. Actually, I'm enjoying the conversation. "Forgive me. But, well, I think this is what you need to know. Do you have any questions"—she pauses for a split second, checks the file with my name, and enunciates emphatically—"Ian?"

"What's that over there?"

I point to a poster with an infographic of a pregnant woman titled HIV AND PREGNANCY: IT'S POSSIBLE.

"Ah, so you want to be a father someday?" she asks.

"Uh . . . no. Unless I adopt a kid with my future husband."

She smiles, and I feel a comfortable warmth in my chest, because it's not a condescending smile nor one with a judgmental undertone.

"Well, if at any point you change your mind and decide to have a biological child, it's entirely possible to have one with proper planning, without the baby contracting the virus through either the father's semen or the mother's bloodstream. In fact, the treatment is very effective, as long as it's followed to the letter. Just like every other treatment we offer here."

It's not that I had been seriously thinking about having children, but this information somehow makes me a little happier.

"And how do I get the medication?" I ask, changing the subject.

Maybe this is my biggest fear, more than the idea of dying in the near future. I'm not thrilled at the idea of depending on public services, let alone the public health system. Everything I see on TV says that nothing works, that lines go on for miles, that medicine is lacking, and that people are always at the mercy of medical professionals who are often not that concerned with the well-being of others. But this conversation shows me that maybe the news isn't always right about health care.

"As I said, everything is very effective."

"How effective?" I ask skeptically.

"Look: Sometimes we might run out of medicine for hypertension at our pharmacy, but in my eight years working here, we've never run out of antiretroviral medication."

"Not even once?"

"Not even once."

That sounds like good news, at least.

"Any other questions?"

"Not for now, but I'm sure I'll have more in the future."

"I hope you do. Well, I think that's it, then." She hands me a paper with an exam request. "This is for blood exams so we can confirm the serology, to get your viral load count and level of CD4, which are your body's defense cells. When you exit, just stop by the lab on the other side of the hall to have your blood drawn. Do you have a phone number where I can reach you?"

I give her my cell phone number because I don't want any

health-care professionals calling my home, only to have my mom pick up and start asking questions.

She writes down the number and then shows me another, a four-digit sequence in her perfectly round handwriting next to my picture.

"This is your medical record number," she says, pointing at 6438. "You can use this number for anything that requires an ID here, particularly for the meds at the pharmacy."

"And do I start taking those today?"

"Not yet. First you need to consult with the doctor and do a blood test to determine your CD4 levels and viral load count, so we can track the medication's progress and its efficacy in your body. I see you're having your consultation tomorrow, but I'll go ahead and schedule the next visit for . . ." She opens up a yellow notebook and checks the calendar. "Does next week work for you? What time of day is best?"

"In the afternoon is best, if that's okay."

She nods and writes down an appointment for two o'clock, five days from now, which works well, because it means I don't have to skip class or make up a bad excuse, since I can come straight from school and just say that I was at the library studying late.

"So that's it." Fernanda gets up and reaches out for a handshake. I grab my backpack from the floor and put it on. "The road ahead won't be short, nor does it have a clear end, but believe me when I say your life can be as normal as anyone else's. The difference is that, from now on, you'll be required to have regular blood work done and take good care of yourself, which everyone should be doing anyway."

"Right," I say, shaking her hand and heading toward the door, feeling the hot air rush in when I open it. "Thank you for everything, Fernanda."

"Take care, Iago," she says with a smile.

# CHAPTER 5

# VICTOR

OUR LINGUISTIC ANTHROPOLOGY PROFESSOR is the type who just sits there with a textbook open in front of him for the entire class, pointing things out while he reads a few lines and thinks this is an effective teaching method for a university. Honestly, what the hell was I thinking when I decided that being a film major would be a good idea?

Sandra is sitting next to me, and she wants nothing more than to be anywhere but here. She tries to focus on her Kindle, which is propped behind the chair of the girl sitting in front of her so the professor can't see what she's up to. Not that he cares, of course.

Annoyed at all this dull blabbering—the seniors say all you have to do on the exam is write something complicated between quotation marks and attribute it to Lévi-Strauss, since rumor has it that the professor never checks whether the reference is real or not anyway—I get up and leave the classroom, the door groaning behind me.

Outside, dozens of students from other classes are chatting, sipping coffee, and smoking, some cutting class, others waiting for theirs to begin. The Institute of Art and Social Communication at Fluminense Federal University is right across from the most popular square in the city of Niterói, a place well known for its social gatherings abounding with beer, weed, cigarettes, and loud music. It's a dangerous street, which means students learn quickly to walk in groups in and out of the main gate, even this early in the morning.

The campus's walls are a kaleidoscope of different colors and art styles, covered in signs for film circuits, live stage performances, and art exhibits, as well as grafitti and artistic depictions of feminism and gender equality. Wood benches are spread out around the courtyard, and I sit down on one of them, checking my phone to see how much more time I have of this torturous class.

"Dear Lord, I didn't think anyone was going to muster up the courage to leave." Sandra comes out right behind me, pulling a pack of cigarettes from her pocket and lighting one. She's five feet tall and one hundred fifty pounds, and she wears a thin layer of makeup on her face at all times, which makes her look radiant. Of course, the purple beret and red hair make her look like Judy Funnie from *Doug*. She's a walking film major cliché, holding the cigarette with the tip of her fingers and doling out ironic comments and sharp opinions. "Want one?"

"I quit," I say, trying to convince myself that burning some nicotine isn't worth it. Sandra shrugs, puts the pack away, and sits down beside me, watching as I stare at my phone.

"Any news from the boy?"

She's talking about Henrique, but he's not the one on my mind right now.

It's been two days since I was at the clinic and gave my number to Ian, the guy at the bus stop, but he still hasn't reached out to me. I've spent way too much time asking myself if he's okay, if he needs some kind of help.

"He apologized, and I tried to start a conversation, but maybe we don't have a future together," I say, talking about Henrique.

"And that's not your prejudice talking, right?"

"Prejudice?"

"Yeah. He's positive and you're not . . . *That* prejudice."

"I'd hardly consider that prejudice, Sandra. I'm just being cautious."

"You're avoiding getting to know someone who, if I remember correctly, was the most interesting guy you'd met in a long time. Your words, not mine."

I brush my blue streak behind my ear, away from my eye.

Sandra smiles.

"I know, but it's . . . complicated," I answer.

"Victor, you're six feet tall, one hundred fifty pounds, and gay, with blue hair that you say you dyed because you want to express yourself, but you make a point of dressing like a preppy law student who was raised by his Catholic grandmother." She's pointing out that I'm the only one here wearing a polo shirt, jeans, and leather shoes. "*You're* complicated."

I roll my eyes, and she leans her head on my arm as I let out a sigh, trying not to think about how true that statement is—I *am* complicated. Instead, I focus on Henrique and the fact that I don't know if I want to be just friends with him. He's an incredible guy, and even though I only met him a few weeks ago, I can't help but feel that this thing between us is more than *just* friendship. Call it chemistry, if you will.

I want to say, "I never thought a date from Tinder could affect me like this. I mean, what are the odds?"

But I'd never admit that to Sandra, because in a way, she's right. I don't know if the correct word is *prejudice*, exactly, but the stuff you hear about HIV is so terrifying that I don't know if I want to live forever in fear that, sooner or later, something might end up happening to me. I can't even begin to imagine what it's like to live with the virus, and I don't know if I'd be strong enough to have it for the rest of my life.

At the same time, these last few days were important for me as I learned a little more about what the hell this thing is that everyone is afraid of and how it manifests in the body. I got a bit obsessed, doing research in Incognito mode so I wouldn't leave a trace of my keywords on the computer. I browsed videos made by HIV-positive people, read testimonials, and even watched a documentary that showed how different things are now from when the epidemic first started, when everything was breaking news. How people would associate HIV and AIDS with being gay and nicknamed the disease "gay cancer" and "gay plague." How they said it was God's punishment, and how an entire generation, already fragile from all the prejudice of a macho, conservative society, perished overnight.

But I also saw hope: how treatment has advanced over time, and how people have been able to pick themselves up after so many deaths and so much suffering. During the process, I learned new words—like *serology, serodiscordant, seroconcordant, undetectable, PEP, PrEP, Truvada, Efavirenz, viral load,* and *CD4 count*—looking up the definition of each and trying to understand what it meant.

I read terrible things and felt a lump in my throat every time I stumbled upon another devastating article. I learned of cases where people, revolted by their own condition, decided not to get treatment and believed that spreading the virus was the best way to get rid of their own negative thoughts. I saw people who were harassed after opening up about their positive status, and others who've refused treatment and are waiting for the virus to progress in their bodies so they'll die, because they don't think life is worth living after testing positive.

Even if Henrique told me he's getting treated and is undetectable, can I believe him? Can I trust that he's telling the truth, or is he one of those people who says one thing but does another? How can I know what kind of person he really is?

"I think you could allow yourself to have a conversation with him," Sandra says. "Who knows—even if nothing happens, what's the harm if you become friends?"

"I don't know," I say as all these thoughts swirl in my head. "I don't think he wants to be just friends."

"Maybe *you* don't want to be just friends."

She knows me way too well.

"Maybe," I admit.

"The big problem with fear, my friend, is that while it helps to keep us from getting screwed, it's also the enemy of happiness."

"Since when are you such a philosopher?"

"Since you started needing advice from someone who finds being happy to be a good thing. Promise me you'll think about it?"

I ponder it for a few seconds in silence and finally answer: "I promise."

It's not as if I haven't already been thinking about it for the last few days.

+

I get a text from an unknown number around lunchtime, when I'm eating at Miss Irene's food truck with Sandra.

Unknown sender:

> Hey, remember me?

> What's the guy with the sad songs called again? I'm in dire need of more depressing songs in my life, and I've had enough of Lana Del Rey.

I smile, then add Ian to my contacts.

"What's up?" asks Sandra, looking at my expression. "Is that Henrique?"

"No, another friend," I answer as I type my reply.

Victor:

Johnny Hooker.

How're you doing?

He answers right away.

Ian:

Scared.

Tired.

Annoyed.

Victor:

That's a lot of feelings for just one person.

Ian:

You have no idea.

Victor:

I didn't think you were gonna text me.

Ian:

I wasn't going to, actually.

Idk, didn't want to bother anyone with my problems, and you don't even know me.

You must be thinking all kinds of stuff about me.

Victor:

If I thought you were going to be a bother . . . I would've given you a pat on the back and walked away. Have you talked to anyone about your results yet?

Ian:

No.

Working up the courage to tell my best friend.

Victor:

Why?

You think he'll freak out?

Ian:

Idk, I'm scared something will change.

Victor:

If it does, then he's not your best friend.

Ian:

Good point.

Victor:

Do you want me to put you in touch with that friend I told you about?

I talked to him, he said it's fine.

You don't know each other.

> So at least you don't have to worry about him judging you.

> Could be good for you.

> He's cool.

The messages say Read right away, but his answer takes some time. A balloon pops up with an ellipsis, indicating that he's typing, then disappears, appears again, disappears, and appears one more time, as if Ian were writing the first book of the Old Testament with his fingertips.

I can almost see his brown eyes as he contemplates whether contacting Henrique is a good idea or not. And when the answer appears, it's only two sentences long.

Ian:

> Maybe.

> But, like . . . I wouldn't be bothering him?

> Victor:

> If you are, he can block your number.

> But I doubt he would.

> Sometimes people like to help without expecting anything in return.

> You should try to let yourself be helped.

It's so much easier to offer advice when you're not the one who needs it.

"What's with all the typing?" Sandra asks, annoyed with my silence and my eyes being glued to the screen. "You're really not talking to Henrique, right? Because if you are and won't show me, I swear our friendship will be hanging by a thread!"

"It's not Henrique!" I smile and show her Ian's name and picture on my phone.

"Whoa, you get over your exes quickly."

"He's just a friend, I swear!" I answer.

"Right . . ."

I turn my attention back to the phone and read the last message from Ian while Sandra goes back to eating her lunch.

Ian:

Hey, you barely know me!

Victor:

If I tell you a secret, can you keep it to yourself?

Ian:

I'm now an Olympic secret keeper.

Yours is safe with me.

Victor:

I can read people's minds.

And I know you're the type who hates accepting help.

Whether for practical reasons or emotional support.

Ian:

And you figured that out just by reading my mind?

Victor:

Of course I did.

Ian:

Most frauds who say they can read minds rely on common sense.

Like, when a guy says, "I see you are suffering because of a family issue."

Hard to find someone without family issues.

I laugh, which makes Sandra look my way again. She raises an eyebrow and goes back to her food in silence.

Victor:

Believe whatever you want.

I can read minds.

Period.

Ian:

Fine, then, Sookie Stackhouse.

Thanks for chatting with me.

I really needed it.

I send him Henrique's contact info.

Victor:

My friend's number. His name is Henrique.

Talk to him and see what he has to say.

Ian:

Could be a good idea.

Victor:

You're a cool guy.

:)

Ian:

I'm sure Henrique thinks the same about you.

Are you guys, like, dating?

The question makes me uncomfortable, but the great advantage of texting is that the person on the other side can't see your expression.

Victor:

It's complicated.

Ian:

He's positive, and you're not.

If we were playing chess, this would be checkmate.

Victor:

I'm sorry.

I don't want you to think I'm insensitive.

Ian:

No worries.

I'll try to talk to him.

And we can chat more later.

A little later, he adds:

Ian:

Oh, and thank you so much.

Victor:

I'm the one who should be thanking you.

Ian:

For what?

Crying on your shoulder?

Victor:

Of course not.

Ian:

Then for what?

**Victor:**

It's complicated.

:)

**Ian:**

Has anyone ever told you that you're complicated?

**Victor:**

Believe it or not . . .

You're the second person to tell me so just today.

**Ian:**

Once is chance, two times is a coincidence, three times is a pattern.

At least that's what they say about serial killers.

**Victor:**

I hope there's no third time.

Or I'll start worrying.

I lock the phone and shove it in my pocket.

"Finally!" Sandra grumbles when I look at my food, basically untouched and now cold. "If you've found a new best friend, you better tell me right now. It'll save me a lot of time I'd need to spend searching for a new one."

"And *I'm* the dramatic one," I answer, cutting a piece of steak and eating a forkful.

# CHAPTER 6

# HENRIQUE

I'M ON A CROWDED BUS heading toward central Rio, squeezed between one man who doesn't know the concept of personal hygiene and another who wears an exhausted expression, his hands holding on to the metal rail and his head resting against his own shoulder, as if praying silently for someone to let him sit down so he can sleep a bit before he gets home. My head starts throbbing, and when I try to distract myself with my phone, I notice a text from an unknown number. At first I think it might be a mistake, but as soon as I read it, I realize who it is.

Unknown number:

Hi, we haven't met, but Victor gave me your number and said we could chat.

I consider whether or not I should get back to him. I wonder if it would be better to let the conversation die right now instead of getting involved with someone I don't even know. Why did I let Eric say it was okay for a stranger to get in touch with me? Why am I making so many concessions to Victor when he doesn't want anything to do with me? I'm no good for him, but good enough to act as a therapist to someone he just met?

At the same time, I know this guy must be terrified. I've been through all this and know how gravity seems off-kilter when there's so much running through your mind. If I can help him feel better, why should I refuse to? If I'd had somebody to tell me everything would be okay, would I have had to spend so many sleepless nights with my face buried in my pillow, choking back screams and tears?

I remember that, when I was diagnosed, I wanted nothing more than someone to talk to, and the prospect of talking to a complete stranger had started to seem like a viable possibility. I had tried an online HIV support group, but I didn't like how easy it was for people to remain anonymous online, and most people there would only share how much they wanted to find out who had given them the virus so they could get their revenge but felt exempt from their own responsibility in it.

It wasn't a good idea. I spent way too much time consumed by all that negativity before finally giving up and trying a different approach, which included Eric and the fear that I had of telling him about my diagnosis.

At the time, we were already sharing our small apartment in Lapa, the result of a bond that stemmed from our similar family histories: My parents couldn't come to terms with the fact that I wouldn't give them grandchildren (unless they were adopted) and that I wouldn't have the traditional church wedding of my mom's dreams, and Eric, a free spirit who found in drag a form of artistic expression—one that his father considered shameful—got kicked out of the house after his mother died.

Telling Eric about my test results was less traumatizing than I imagined. When something as scary as a chronic virus appears in our lives, we get all sorts of negative thoughts, and the first one is that, somehow, people will look at us differently. That they will avoid us, won't hug us the way they used to anymore. So when I finally mustered up the courage and showed Eric the slip of paper with the damn X next to *HIV+*, I don't really know what I expected. Maybe that he'd be disappointed, maybe that he would start screaming and want to move out, or that he would give me a hug and console me, as if I were on the brink of death.

But he did something else: He just shrugged, gave me back the paper, and asked if I had already started treatment. Afterward he went to the kitchen, opened the cabinets, and started preparing a ham-and-cheese lasagna.

"When my mom was alive, she always said there's no bit of bad news that can survive a good lasagna. That was when I told her I was gay, both of us knew that my dad wouldn't like the news, and the cancer was already eating her away. We knew it wouldn't be easy, so that's what she did for me. And that's exactly what I want to tell you: It won't be easy, but we'll always have lasagna."

That was more or less the part where I started crying and hugged him, because I was so thankful to have him in my life. And also because I was hungry.

But what about this Ian guy? Does he have anyone who can make him a lasagna, hug him, and tell him everything is going to be okay? Is he prepared to face the psychological torture that seems to consume you until you finally gather the courage and decide to share the weight of the discovery with someone you love and who will support you? He's probably as confused as I was those first few days, not quite knowing what was happening or how life could keep on being wonderful, even with all its highs and lows.

I add Ian's number to my contacts, trying to find my balance among the people pressing against me on the bus, then start typing.

Henrique:

Hi! Of course we can talk. My name's Henrique, nice to meet you. How's everything?

Ian:

Confusing.

Henrique:

I can imagine. Maybe it's best if we talk in person instead?

Ian:

Do you have the time?

Henrique:

We'll make time. Where do you live?

Ian:

Botafogo, you?

Henrique:

Lapa, but I'm not far from Botafogo.

Ian:

Do you have some time now?

I'm tired and want nothing more than to get home so I can finish *Orange Is the New Black*. Before I can answer, he sends another message.

Ian:

If not, that's okay. We can do it some other time. I don't want to be a bother.

I let out a weary sigh. When people don't know each other, they tend to avoid the first meet-up, and I know from experience that he must be as uncomfortable as I am about this. If there were another way out, he'd be focusing on it. If he wants to meet in person so urgently, he's probably doing very badly.

Henrique:

You're not a bother at all! I'm free. Where can we meet?

Ian:

How about the Botafogo Beach Mall?

Henrique:

Great. Meet you there in . . . what? Half an hour?

Ian:

Okay. Starbucks?

Henrique:

See you there.

Ian:

Thank you.

I slide the phone back into my pocket and press the stop button. I squeeze between the people tired from their workdays, exit the bus, and start my walk toward the subway.

+

I recognize Ian right away from his shaved head and full beard, just like the picture he sent me. He's sitting at a two-seat table with two coffees in front of him, and I notice that one of his legs is

57

bouncing up and down. He seems impatient and uncomfortable. When he sees me approach, he smiles.

"I didn't know what you like, so I ordered a regular coffee with milk," he says, sliding one of the cups toward me. Next to the cup, there are little packets of all the types of sugar and sweeteners available at Starbucks. I grab a Splenda, open the lid of my coffee, and pour it into the liquid, mixing with the wood stirrer.

"You didn't have to do this," I say, delighted by his kindness, then sip the beverage and enjoy the refreshing sensation down my throat. "It's delicious."

"Oh, and I added a little bit of mint."

"I've never tried that. It's good."

He smiles. I put my backpack on my lap and stare at him, not really knowing how to start a conversation with someone I don't know. I have a degree in design, for God's sake, not psychology.

"So . . ." I begin, trying to establish a modicum of intimacy before entering the conversation, because I think that's what he expects. He looks younger than me, and it's a truth universally acknowledged that the eldest are wiser and therefore should lead the way. I think. "I don't want to ask again how things are, because you already said they're confusing, but . . . how are you dealing with all of it?"

He flashes an awkward smile, because he also doesn't really seem to know how to start the conversation, especially with someone he doesn't know. This is starting to feel like a job interview.

An agonizing job interview.

"Everything is so new," he tries to summarize.

"And scary."

"And scary," he echoes, nodding. "But it's not the end of the world, is it?"

"It just looks like it," I say with a smile. I take another sip of the coffee. "But no, it's not the end of the world. I mean, look at me: I'm alive, right? A few episodes of that summertime sadness and a well of irony, but I'm here, and that's all that matters."

"Is it hard?" he asks, and I notice his voice is soft because he doesn't want anyone around to listen to our conversation. So I lower mine, too, and I'm sure we look like two revolutionary leaders conspiring to overthrow a totalitarian regime.

"Depends on what you see as hard. It's annoying, draining, and exhausting . . . but *hard* is a really strong word. Maybe psychologically hard. Physically, only once in a while."

"I'm sorry, I . . ." Ian breathes heavily, and he takes another sip of his coffee, trying to get his thoughts back on track. But he doesn't manage to say anything else.

"You're scared." I say what's on his mind, and he agrees. "Scared of what other people will say, scared of what your life is going to look like from now on, scared that you will be rejected, and scared of all the things you'll need to put into perspective because of this virus. Am I right?"

"Spot on."

"I know what it's like." From the outside, I might seem like the HIV guru who has already overcome all these fears, but they are still here, hidden somewhere. Ian doesn't need to know that, though.

Silence takes over our table, as if the words were gunshots, capable of hitting someone right in the forehead, splattering brains and bone all over the place.

I try to focus on being the hard-and-wise older person at the table and keep talking. "Say what you're thinking. No restrictions. We don't even know each other, so if I pass judgment, you have nothing to worry about. Not that I will, of course. I'm not that kind of person."

He smiles again and looks me right in the eye. It usually bothers me when someone does that, but his brown eyes seem so innocent and well-intentioned at the same time that I don't mind it, because I know he's not trying to decipher me.

"I'm thinking that I could have been more careful, and everything could have been different."

"And also that it wouldn't be a bad idea to have a time machine so you could go back to when you had unprotected sex and knock down the bedroom door and yell, 'Don't do it!'"

"That's about it." He smiles.

"It's not very healthy to think about the impossible."

"It's inevitable."

"You know what I thought when I got my results?" I ask.

"What?"

"That I should have been more careful, and everything could have been different. And that time machines should definitely have already been invented."

He smiles again. "It's bizarre, isn't it?" Ian asks, grabbing his coffee cup with both hands and swirling it around the table.

Uneasy, uncomfortable, unsettled. "We know exactly what to do, but then we think it will never happen to us, until it does. And then we blame ourselves, thinking that everything could have been different."

"We think we're a bizarre kind of superhero, and that the stories we hear don't happen in real life. As if HIV were a big collective delirium that only happens to people in sad movies that get nominated for Oscars," I add. "But this isn't about blame. We only blame ourselves for a little while. I know it's all very recent for you, Ian, but that feeling will go away eventually, or at least you'll find a way to tuck it back in a corner of your mind. Because, in the end, it is not about blame."

"For you, what's been the worst part?" he asks.

"My mind. Definitely my mind and the things that it creates out of my fears. They never go away, you know?" He nods. I keep talking. "Maybe that's the biggest lie in the history of lies that the doctors tell you to make you feel better. They say, 'You get used to it with time. In time, you don't even remember that you have the virus, because you become undetectable, and your odds of transmitting it are zero, and the side effects of the medicine aren't as bad, and you take your pill automatically. As if it were for high blood pressure. As if it were for diabetes.'" I let out a dry laugh. "But it's a lie, at least for me. Not a single day goes by when I don't remember the virus, and not one goes by when I don't worry that I'm not exactly like everyone else anymore."

Ian looks at me attentively.

"I'm sorry, I . . ." I smile humorlessly, running my hands over my red hair in an attempt to tame it. "I should be trying to make you feel better, and look at what I'm doing."

"It's not a problem. It's great that someone is being honest, for a change."

"Doctors only *think* they know what happens in here," I say, pointing at my own head. "And of course we process it all in our own way. When I have doctors' appointments, I meet a lot of people in the waiting rooms, and one thing I've learned is that we each view the virus—and life with the virus—differently. I met a woman who got it from her husband because he was cheating on her, but she forgave him and was pregnant, on treatment so the child would be born without the virus. And a forty-five-year-old man, father to a fifteen-year-old girl, with enough money to travel wherever he wanted every six months. When we talked, he seemed determined to make things work and said that he didn't want to give up on life, that he loved to see the world, and that his diagnosis had given him a new perspective on how much he could still enjoy. Then he stopped coming to the clinic, and one day I saw on the news that he had jumped from a twelfth-floor window." I shrug. "The thing is, even with all the information out there, people are still shitting themselves with fear of having something like this in their lives, but everyone responds to bad news in a different way."

"And how did you take the bad news?" he asks.

I look away from him for a few seconds and gaze at the name scribbled on the side of the coffee cup next to a smile that the barista drew.

I try to organize my thoughts.

"At first, I had this fixed idea that the clinic had screwed up my blood test and that the reagent they had used had gone bad." I laugh when I remember how that coping mechanism had seemed like the easiest at the time. I scratch my cheek and feel my unkempt beard poking the tips of my fingers. "I redid the test at a private lab, and it also came back positive. So I started thinking that the private lab was wrong and went to another and took the test again. When I realized it was not a bad joke or a collective mistake, I started thinking about what I had to do. I read a lot about the history of the virus and decided that not taking care of myself would be stupid, so I started treatment."

"Did you have any side effects?"

"A few, but nothing I couldn't get over. There's a medicine that most people take, and it affects your nervous system, so I had a lot of nightmares at first, and my moods were unpredictable. Sometimes I'd blow up at my roommate because he'd leave his wigs around the living room, and then I would start crying because I thought I'd hurt the only friend I had and he'd never want to see my face again." I laugh one more time, which makes Ian laugh as well. I must seem totally out of balance. "And once in a while, the bad thoughts still happen, but we learn to hide how we feel. Because it's almost always just the medicine lying to us and messing with our heads, making us believe that nobody cares, when in fact a lot of people do care."

"And does anyone know about you?" he asks.

"My friend with all the wigs, who's the best person in the

universe," I answer with a smile. "His name is Eric, and he does drag."

"And Victor," he adds, when he realizes I don't include anyone else.

"And Victor," I echo, and I'm sure he notices the annoyed tone in my voice.

"What's going on between the two of you?"

I shake my head to express all the doubts I have about him. "Things are always good up until the Big Reveal. That's when everyone withdraws. But I'm already used to it."

My words sound bitter, which Ian notices.

"It sounds like you've had more than one disappointment."

"That's the bad part of the virus: You never know how someone is going to react. I've heard stories of some who handle being in serodiscordant relationships very well, and I wish I were one of those people who could tell you that the virus isn't a problem and I found the love of my life, but I haven't been very lucky over the last three years."

"So Victor's wasn't the first negative reaction you've faced?"

"It wasn't, but I always wonder if it's a good idea to tell the people I'm into about my status. I take every precaution and consider my responsibility in all this, but at the same time, I don't know if it's fair not to talk about it, you know? Not talking only feeds into fear and prejudice."

"And you like Victor?"

I find it difficult to answer.

"He's a cool guy, and we have a lot in common, but I'm always a bit frustrated by the negative reactions, even though I know they exist."

"That doesn't answer my question."

"For someone I just met, you're pretty incisive," I say.

"I'm sorry, I didn't—"

"It's okay, I don't mind talking about it." I smile. "Well, if you're looking for a yes or no, I'll say yes, I like him. But not the reaction."

"His or in general?"

"In general. I think it's a defense mechanism, you know—that I don't let myself get too attached to someone so I don't get hurt later, because it has happened once and I don't want it to happen again."

Carlos suddenly invades my thoughts. That moron.

"Any particular post–Big Reveal disappointments?" Ian seems interested in my life, and I notice his body tilting forward a little, and that his left elbow is propped against the table. He's like a child in a library, anxiously awaiting the story.

I'm not sure why, but his interested expression makes me laugh. Not one of the dry laughs that echoes in the back of your throat and feels more like disdain, but one with a full-toothed smile, with tears in your eyes and ragged breath.

He realizes what is happening and moves his elbow away from the table, shoving his hands between his legs.

"I'm sorry, I didn't mean to . . . overstep," he says, embarrassed.

"I told you I don't mind. You seem like the kind of person who feels good hearing about other people's tragedies, am I right?" I don't mean it as a criticism, and he can tell that by the humor in my voice.

"*Game of Thrones* is my favorite TV show. I love a little bit of tragedy."

"*Game of Thrones* is such a cliché. You should try some Russian literature if you're looking for real tragedy. Or *The Boy in the Striped Pajamas*, for something shorter."

"*Game of Thrones* has dragons. It's cooler."

"Okay, one should not discuss matters of taste, as my mom would say. But as for my own tragedy, which is much more important than any beheadings in Westeros—"

"So you *do* watch *Game of Thrones*!"

"Focus!" I snap my fingers, and he smiles. "As for my tragedy: It involves a boy and another fantasy world, but this one was shot in New Zealand . . ."

"What does *The Lord of the Rings* have to do with the story?"

"My ex was crazy about Tolkien and those movies. I was, too, but when things went south between us, I never managed to look at Gandalf's face again without thinking of him as an old asshole, even though I know he has nothing to do with my problems."

"And that was one of the guys who disappeared after the Big Reveal?"

"Not quite like that, and that's what hurt the most," I say, trying to ignore the memory of Carlos's hazel eyes and his straw-colored hair, and the birthmark hidden on his cheek, right beneath the thick blond beard that he insisted on growing, even though I hated it. "I found out I had HIV when I was with him. We were a weird duo, because while I was already not living with my parents anymore and felt pretty at peace with my sexuality, he had a serious complex, wouldn't come out to anyone because of his military father and religious mother, and was afraid to leave the nest and take on the world. Ours was one of those relationships you had to hide behind the facade of friendship, you know? But, anyway, we went to get tested together, that whole thing of boyfriends ready to take our commitment to the next level, because I kept insisting that he needed to come out of the closet and find a way to be happy. Then all my tests came back positive, and his was negative, and he told me he'd still be there to give me all the support I might need. And I felt relieved in that moment, because even if I was in deep shit with this virus, I still had a speck of hope that at least the HIV wouldn't affect that one relationship.

"We'd always used condoms, even before my diagnosis, but I was still worried. He came with me to the first few doctor's appointments, and I insisted he should repeat the test three more times throughout the following year to be sure it was negative. He always told me that, if by any chance one of those results came back positive, nothing would change between us. That we'd go through it together, and all that motivational BS.

"Then the testing cycle was done, and he was sure he didn't have the virus. I'd never been so relieved in my entire life, because I don't ever want to know what it's like to be responsible for having transmitted it to someone. And then after all that time dealing with and talking about HIV, doing a lot of research about the virus and even going to counseling together to discuss it with a therapist, he just disappeared. Poof, like smoke. He wouldn't pick up my calls, would see my texts and not get back to me. When I finally worked up the courage to go to his place, his parents opened the door with suspicious looks. All they knew about me was that Carlos and I were friends, but they wanted to know my name. They recognized me from photos, all with other people in them, too, because Carlos thought photos of just the two of us together would make people talk. So his mother told me he'd gone to New Zealand to study abroad. She asked me if I'd known he was going, and she thought it was weird when I said no, because he'd been saving the money for eight months and bought the ticket way in advance. His dad even added, proudly, that Carlos had said he was exchanging letters with a girl in the program, and that the two of them were probably meeting up and bound to start a relationship. Of course, I didn't say anything, but I wavered between laughter and shock, because his dad seemed like he bought the story about an international girlfriend.

"I couldn't understand why he'd been so dishonest with me, but I took a deep breath and spent the next two days writing him a long email, saying that I'd been to his place and found out about New Zealand. The bastard replied with a photo about a week later. It seemed I was just one among his many friends. The message was impersonal, like one of those that you copy and paste to all of your contacts, saying that he missed me but it was time for a change, and that he was really happy with the decision. He added that he'd changed his phone number, so he was sorry if I'd tried to call him or sent texts he wasn't able to answer."

I take a sip of my coffee that's already cold, my throat welcoming the liquid after all this talking. I notice that Ian hasn't blinked since I stopped for a breath.

"What a huge asshole . . ." he mumbles, mouth agape.

"Yeah. Needless to say, I spent the rest of the year teary-eyed and feeling sorry for myself. It was the worst experience I've had in my life. Honestly, it was worse than the HIV bombshell. Because I trusted him and thought we'd have a lasting relationship, you know? We had plans to move to São Paulo or somewhere in the Northeast after college, and he just threw a smoke bomb and disappeared like the Wicked Witch of the West.

"After that happened, I became completely closed off to relationships. I went for more than a year without sex, and I'd barely ever go out to meet new people. Eric, my roommate, performs in some shows downtown and would always pester me to come with him. He'd bring people over to our place to get them to talk to me so I could make new friends, but I had hit rock bottom. I had crying fits out of nowhere at weird times. If I was at work and felt one of them coming, I'd hide in the bathroom and stay there, sobbing until I managed to calm down; if I was on the bus, I'd put on my sunglasses, even at night, and close my eyes, trying to take deep breaths and think good thoughts. It was a terrible time in my life, and once in a while the feeling of despair still comes back, you know, because we get used to the medicine, but sometimes it still gets the best of you."

"And how did you get over all of that?"

"I burned my copies of the Lord of the Rings trilogy in a ritual with Eric dressed in a Galadriel costume. *The Hobbit* had to go, too, as did the DVDs of all the movies. It was the breakup moment, you know, and ended up being funny because Eric memorized the scene from *The Fellowship of the Ring* where Galadriel bellows, 'ALL SHALL LOVE ME AND DESPAAAAIR,'" I say, shaking my arms in the middle of the coffee shop, my eyes wide, which makes Ian let out a good-humored laugh. "After that, I decided it made much more sense to appreciate the people who'd do that kind of thing for me, instead of a douchebag who disappeared without a trace."

"I think that's an excellent decision."

"And you know the worst part? New Zealand has restrictions for HIV immigration. I don't know if he knew about that or not when he went there, but it only made me more pissed about the whole thing. And this kind of stuff leaves a scar. Since Carlos, I haven't been able to trust people the same way. I only trust who I already know, you know? I'm always hesitant when I'm about to start something new, whether it's a friendship or with a love inter-est, and I think that's the worst way to go about it. But I can't help myself."

"You're talking to me, a complete stranger," Ian points out, shrugging.

"That's exactly *why*. I can just walk out of here and never reply to any other text from you, block you on every app there is, and go on with my life as if nothing ever happened."

"Are you going to?"

"You're a cool guy. And you probably have a lot ahead of you when you start taking the medicine. So I'll give you the benefit of the doubt and keep the communication channels open."

"Hey, that's progress, right?"

I take a last sip of my coffee. Colder than Winterfell.

"Maybe it is."

Ian gives me a satisfied smile and says, "I know I've barely said anything about myself, but I wanted to tell you that this . . . this conversation . . . was so helpful to me. For real. And I know that I'm just a stranger hearing about all of this from the outside, but I still want to offer a piece of advice: Be persistent with Victor. You seem to like him, and he seems to like you. Maybe things aren't that clear, but I'm sure that, at the very least, he'll take the time to listen to you. Even if it doesn't go anywhere, it doesn't hurt to try, does it?"

I take in his advice.

"Maybe" is all I can muster.

Ian gets up, ready to leave. And then, on a whim, I ask: "Do you like nightclubs?"

"Like, with country music and people spilling cheap whiskey on the floor?"

"Dear Lord, what kind of nightclubs have you been going to?"

"My friends took me to one once. It was awful."

"My darling, I'm talking drag queens and Beyoncé the whole night. And buy-one-get-one-free beer."

"Is there such a place?"

"That's where Eric performs." Then I try to make it clear that I'm not hitting on him. "Look, I know this post-diagnosis time is super awful, so I think you should leave the house for a bit, even if it's just to listen to some loud music and end up smelling like cigarette smoke. Getting out of your own head is good once in a while. And Eric is preparing a Cleopatra performance for the next show. It's this weekend. Are you in?"

"Why not?" he answers with a smile. "Send me the address and the date, and I'll stop by."

We both get up, and our smiles are strong indicators that this conversation isn't over yet. Somehow, I know we just planted a little seed of friendship.

He raises his hand to shake mine, but before I notice it, I'm already hugging him like we're friends who ran into each other after a long time apart.

"I really appreciate you taking the time to talk to me, Henrique. It did me good."

I only nod in response.

Maybe I don't want to admit it out loud, but the conversation was good for me, too.

# CHAPTER 7

# IAN

I STILL DON'T KNOW HOW to feel about my conversation with Henrique. Somehow, listening to other people's problems makes things seem less complicated, or at least helps me to rationalize them from another perspective. But in the end, they're just words.

When I get home, it feels like family night: My mom has taken over the living room table with her blueprints, her endless supply of coffee, and a tuna salad sandwich that she must've made in a hurry. Dad is in the bedroom, hunched over a small desk, grading the exams of students who wouldn't hesitate to beg for extra decimal points in order to avoid spending another two weeks studying to retake them. And Vanessa is lying on the floor of the bedroom that we share, four different textbooks and a notebook open in front of her while her earbuds blast some boring classical music (she says it's the only way she can concentrate in this zoo that we call our home).

I go to the bedroom, put on some old, wrinkled clothes, and plunge into my bed, physically and mentally exhausted from this frantic marathon that I'm trying to be discreet about—of doctors, tears, and conversations with strangers. Vanessa notices I'm not making small talk or trying to disturb her, so she furrows her brow and takes out the earbuds.

"Is everything okay, Ian?"

Her curly hair is tied in a knot on top of her head, an attempt to find some relief from the heat of the night. The ceiling fan turns at full speed, making the curtain flutter. With Vanessa's earbuds removed, I notice the music is too loud, but I can't even bring myself to give one of my acerbic lectures about her going deaf before thirty.

"Just tired," I say, still looking up, feeling my shoulders relax against the mattress. "What are you up to?"

"A project for biology." That explains why she is so hard at work and why the books are so thick. "The teacher asked us to research STIs. I got HIV and AIDS. Did you know they're two different things?"

I grab the pillow from under my head and bury my face in it.

The universe has *got* to be messing with me.

+

My eyes shoot open when my phone rings at ten p.m. Vanessa is still working away on her research, this time with her face glued to her laptop and a thousand tabs open with information about HIV and AIDS. Classical music is blasting from the earbuds, but I'm so distracted that I barely notice Vivaldi has now become the sound-track of our evening.

I check my phone and see that it's Gabriel, my best friend. I leave the bedroom and walk to the kitchen, maybe the only place in my house that doesn't look like a zoo.

"Hello?"

"You didn't answer my texts." The voice on the other side is accusatory, impatient, and, to some extent, amused. "I hope you have a good explanation, and that it involves a phone being stolen or something other than your complete indifference to my concern."

"Good evening to you, too, Gabriel."

"Where are you?"

"It's ten o'clock on a Thursday night. Where do you *think* I am?" I ask. "Obviously, I'm at home."

"Great."

The phone goes silent, and I'm not sure if Gabriel is so mad at me that he decided to hang up or if we just got disconnected.

I try calling him back, but then quickly realize why he's not on the other end of the phone when I hear the doorbell, which catches everyone by surprise.

I go to the living room and see my mother, a frown on her face thanks to an unexpected visitor at this hour as she unlocks the door and opens it. And there's my best friend, with his five-foot-five frame, black skin, and forearms covered with tattoos. From a distance, Gabriel could pass for sixteen, but he's about to turn

75

twenty-one. It's as if he drinks some kind of potion brewed by a witch who drains the youth from unsuspecting children and gathers it up in little plastic bottles.

"Hi, Mrs. Gonçalves! I just wanted to have a word with Ian."

I appear behind my mother, who flashes a big smile at Gabriel and wraps her arms around him in a hug before letting him in. She lets out a "What a great surprise!" as my dad peeks out of the bedroom and waves at Gabriel, who waves back. The music is so loud in my room that I'm certain Vanessa didn't even hear the bell ring, which is the only reason I can think of that she wouldn't come out to say hello, too.

Gabriel is one of the most welcomed visitors in my house. Maybe the fact that we've been friends for years now plays a part, but certainly not more so than the fact that he's straight. My parents think he's good company and usually don't lecture me at all when I tell them I'm hanging out with him, no matter how late. As if Gabriel could somehow save me from bad influences and convert me to what they consider a "normal lifestyle." Which doesn't really bother me anymore. I got tired of having arguments with my parents that led nowhere, and I figured out that the only way I could maintain a relationship with them was through silence. Silence is the best form of dialogue.

"Do you think you could make some time for your best friend?" He gives me a hug. "Or are you planning on ignoring my texts forever? I'm starving and in the mood for a burger, what do you say?"

Maybe the surprised-yet-dispirited expression on my face is

76

enough for Gabriel to know that something is wrong, and his smile falls into an uncertain frown. Unlike most people, he can read between the lines of all my facial expressions and knows how to differentiate my genuine smiles from the ones I use to hide problems.

It's weird to think that this guy, who is so different from me and all those who surround me, is one of the best people in my life, even if he hasn't been a part of it for very long. We met casually, when his car broke down around the corner from our place. He was 100 percent lost in that overheated piece of scrap metal, and it wasn't even five minutes before my dad realized Gabriel didn't have car insurance and wouldn't be able to afford a tow truck.

Luckily, my dad knows a bit about cars. In half an hour, he popped the hood, poured some water wherever water is supposed to go (I didn't inherit the ability to tell the difference between a motor and a battery, as you can see), and told Gabriel to give it a second and everything would be okay. We were ready to leave, but Gabriel insisted on paying us back somehow, which culminated in the three of us sitting on plastic stools, devouring hot dogs and drinking Guaraná, which was all Gabriel could afford that day.

That could've been the end of it, but we ended up talking for way too long. It was a special day not only because we met him but also because he was the perfect middleman between my dad and me. When Gabriel realized soccer wasn't a shared interest of ours and that I went quiet when he and my dad started going on about the Brazilian championship, he changed the subject. He started talking about how he wanted to go to vet school, and how he was going to take a college prep course, and what I should expect in high school.

What drew me to him, besides the quick realization that he knew how to hold a conversation, was that he didn't treat me as inferior just because I was younger. His words flowed with the kind of honesty you only get from close friends, and I remember thinking, *Whoa, he'd make a great friend.*

Finally, after we said goodbye, I worked up the courage to ask for his number. And maybe there was some kind of ulterior motive at the time, given how fascinated I was by him. But as our conversations progressed from the odd text message here and there to something more regular, and then very frequent, I realized I didn't want anything more than friendship with Gabriel. And also that talking to him was helpful, maybe because he was far away, or perhaps just because I had started to trust him.

After the hellos and Gabriel's several thanks-but-no-thanks to all the food my mom tries to offer, I take him to my room. Vanessa lowers the music volume and smiles when he comes in, and I take off my shorts and worn-out T-shirt to find something more appropriate for an outdoor walk. I remember the time when my sister had a crush on Gabriel and could barely address him without stammering. I'm not sure if it was because he'd always help her with her biology homework or because he was the most stylish and pleasant person she knew. It was more or less around that time that Vanessa started insisting she'd get a tattoo, but my mom forbade her, and the idea died little by little along with her crush on Gabriel.

"I'm not gonna be long!" I tell my parents when I'm done changing and have left the bedroom, opening the front door and shoving my keys in my pocket.

I feel a shiver down my spine, anticipating the conversation I'm about to have. I still don't know if I want to tell him about my diagnosis, and the idea of just saying "Everything is okay" starts taking shape in my head. I don't want to worry my best friend with my problems. Actually, I don't want to *lose* my best friend to my problems, and the fact that I have no idea how he might react only makes me feel worse.

Worse than the silence as we wait for the elevator.

"So," I begin, making conversation. "How's Daniela? Things still good between the two of you?"

He stares at me with a questioning expression, probably trying to determine if I'm stalling for time with irrelevant questions or if I'm actually showing interest in his life.

"We're doing good. She's defending her thesis in March, and mine's in April. Then we'll be done with school, and we can come back to Rio."

"Cool. Are you thinking of moving in together?"

He shrugs. "We haven't talked about it yet. She's nice, and we're happy, but I still haven't decided if I'm ready for that."

The elevator seems stuck somewhere and doesn't come for another few seconds, so we fall silent again. It's the kind of awkward silence that's not supposed to happen between best friends, and I wonder if it's the shadow of my secrets that's making every-thing seem terrible, or if Gabriel and I are so out of touch due to life circumstances that we've become the type of friends who can barely recognize each other when they meet after some time.

"So . . . something's going on." He doesn't ask, just states it, breaking the ice. "Why aren't you talking to me? Why did I have to get in my car and drive all the way to your house so you'd be forced to speak to me?"

"Nothing's going on," I say. Yeah, that might be the best option. The fewer people I bring into the mess that my life has become, the better. "I'm just busy with life, that's all. I'm sorry I didn't get back to you, Gabriel. You didn't have to drive all the way here just for that."

I make a fist and squeeze my thumb into my palm, cracking my knuckle and feeling my eyes sting. *You can't cry right now, Ian. Please, no matter what happens, don't cry. You've already cried way too much over the last few days.*

"That poker face of yours might work on your parents or sister, Ian, but I know you better. What's the matter?"

The elevator arrives, and luckily, Mrs. Lopes from the seventh floor is in it. The subject dies as we say good evening, and we travel down the six floors to the lobby without making a sound.

I interrogate him as soon as we're out of the building. "Why did you come here? I thought you had class this week."

Gabriel started working at a university in Seropédica when he started vet school and now splits his time between managing pig research and studying for his master's. He shouldn't be in Botafogo in the middle of the week, since Seropédica is at least an hour and a half drive from Rio and he only comes in twice a month to see his mother.

"When your best friend stops texting you back and his sister says nothing happened, it means something happened," he answers. "Vanessa told me everything is fine, which leads me to two possible conclusions: You're either tired of our friendship and aren't responding out of laziness, or there's a reason you're avoiding me. And since I know I'm an excellent friend, the type you don't just dismiss for no good reason, I can only assume that the second conclusion is the correct one."

"You talked to Vanessa about me?"

"I talk about you to everybody. It's kind of a hobby when I've had enough of shoving my hand up pigs' anuses." He smiles and changes the subject. "Where do you want to go?"

"I don't know. You abducted me when I was already in bed, so you tell me."

He shoves his hands in his pockets and pulls out the keys to his car—a '96 maroon Fiat Tempra, falling to pieces. We walk to the old tin can and get in.

He doesn't insert the keys to start the car.

"Are we just sitting here waiting for someone to come rob us?" I ask.

"Ian, what's going on?" he asks again, this time more determined and in a lower voice.

My mouth goes suddenly dry; the question is so direct. He looks right at me, and I only know this because I can feel his eyes on me.

I'm looking straight ahead, chewing on the words that threaten to tumble out of my mouth but at the same time refuse to.

"I told you nothing is . . . going on." I try to act rationally but can barely utter those last words. Gabriel notices I choked on them, and my tone of voice couldn't make it any clearer that I'm lying.

But I need to. I don't want to involve him in my problems.

"Man, I hate being the kind of person who needs to drag something out of you, but we know each other well enough for me to know something is wrong. And it's okay if you don't want to tell me, because you have every right to live your own life. But do you remember when you came out to me?"

I can't help chuckling briefly, because I remember perfectly. I thought it would be the hardest conversation I'd ever have in my life. How naive of me.

"You wouldn't pick up the phone for two weeks, and when I finally showed up on your doorstep, you tried to convince me everything was fine. And then the next week, what happened?"

It annoys me remembering how right he was in being so sure things weren't okay, but I remain silent.

"Do you remember what happened the following week?" he asks again.

"Of course I remember," I say unwillingly. "I argued with my parents, then it all came out, and shit hit the fan. I called you crying, of course, which made you come straight from Seropédica, and you got here at two o'clock in the morning."

"Precisely. And I don't want to not be here if things go south again, Ian. And I'm sure things are bad . . . but again, if you can promise me that everything is okay, I'll pretend like this conversation never happened, and we can go get a burger in Copacabana."

I take a deep breath and let it out at once:

"HIV." My voice sounds tired. There is no easy way to say it, no way to make the letters softer or to work around them. I feel the tears welling up in my eyes again. "I found out at the beginning of the week."

We fall silent. I wait for him to start screaming and telling me how reckless I was, that I could have avoided this shit show that my life has become if only I'd taken better care of myself, and that he can't be around somebody who goes off screwing everyone in sight. I can already predict that he'll be the first of many who won't support me, who will stab me and twist the knife without a hint of pity.

Talking to strangers is one thing. Being judged by people you don't know is bearable because, at the end of the day, they're just strangers who will disappear if you don't want to see them again. But it's different when you share something this big with your best friend—the one with so many stories to tell about the two of you, the one who's always there for you when things go bad.

I don't know why my thoughts are so negative. The silence remains, but the next thing I feel is Gabriel's arms wrapping around me. I bury my head in his right shoulder, wanting the stupid tears to stop coming, but I can't help it.

He strokes my hair as my body starts shaking, and no words could be more important than the warmth of this moment—of knowing that, no matter what happened, he's here, holding me tight.

It means the world to me.

"Why didn't you say anything?" he finally asks, and I don't want to raise my eyes to face him.

"I think I was . . . ashamed," I answer, my voice still muffled by the now-damp sleeve of his shirt.

"Ashamed? Ashamed of what?"

"I—I don't know . . . of everything. I couldn't bear it if you looked at me differently."

"You think I would do that?"

"I don't . . . I don't know anything anymore, Gabriel. I am so scared."

He continues to hug me until I calm down.

"I'd never look at you differently, Ian. You could have a highly contagious disease that would kill you in twenty-four hours, and I'd still give you a hug. And that's not the case. How are you feeling?"

"As if nothing is worth it anymore."

"Not a great way to feel."

"I can't help it."

"I don't know a lot about HIV, but I do know it doesn't have to be fatal anymore, right?"

"Everyone tells me that, and I know I'm blowing it out of proportion. But I don't know if they say that just to make me feel better, or if they're trying to say that whatever doesn't kill you will make you suffer."

"You're not blowing it out of proportion, Ian. I have no idea what it must be like to go through something like this. If I could rip that virus out of you, I swear I'd be working on it this very second, but that's not how things work."

"I know."

"But I don't want you to give up on life, either. It's not a death sentence."

"I know that, Gabriel. I know it's possible to have a fulfilling life. I know that if I follow the proper treatment, my life expectancy will be the same as that of someone without the virus. I know that it's just one pill a day and blood tests every three months. But knowing is not the same as feeling. Knowing is not living without the fear that things might go wrong. It doesn't keep me from spending every waking moment thinking about what it's going to be like from now on. What if I want to have a relationship, or want to travel somewhere? What's going to happen if the medicine stops being manufactured? Hell, I never even thought about studying abroad, but who knows if I can even do that anymore? Will I be able to work as a flight attendant or truck driver, or even backpack through South America? Not that I've ever wanted any of those things, but the idea that I might not be able to do them annoys me. I can't stop thinking that my freedom ended the moment the test results came back. Maybe I did something to deserve all this. Today a friend told me that I can't live in New Zealand because they have some kind of restriction against HIV-positive immigrants. I never thought about living in New Zealand, but the fact that this virus took that choice away from me makes me so . . . pissed."

I know I don't sound rational at all in this moment, but I don't care. All I want is to get this virus out of my system. Words keep tumbling out, one on top of the other, no filter, as though I am only now able to spew all my thoughts without holding back my pain or fears.

"And the worst part is that it would all be different if I'd made different choices," I go on. "No one says that, but I know what everyone thinks: They think of what an idiot I was for not using a condom, of how stupid I was for letting one night that wasn't even spent with someone special determine the rest of my life. No one needs to tell me that, because peoples' eyes say everything. That's what the nurse thinks, it's what you think, it's probably what the friend I talked to thinks."

"You can look at things from that negative perspective, Ian," Gabriel responds. "Or you can choose to believe that the people who support you are truly worried and want to see you well. That instead of judging you, they simply *aren't*, and that's the end of it. You think you're the only one to have had sex without a condom in all of human history?" He laughs. "We all screw up on a daily basis, Ian, and we snap out of the guilt or the thought that we deserve the bad things that happen to us along the way. I don't mean that you shouldn't cry or worry about your diagnosis, but try to look at it as a fact of life, not a punishment. You are the best person I know, man, and I'm sure you don't deserve this. But bad things happen to good people. There's no retributive system. Things just are what they are."

"But it's so . . . hard."

"I know. Or, I can imagine. But life goes on. You're still the same person I met on that day my car broke down and your dad stopped to give me a hand. To me, you're the same guy who dreams of living without money problems and who's planning on becoming an economist for the Central Bank of Brazil; you're still here, right by my side, even if you have a weird knack for numbers and mathematical formulas that I'll never understand. And you can still do everything you want, Ian. If you want to go live in fucking New Zealand, I know you can figure it out, because that's just the kind of person you are, period. This virus is not going to end your life. First of all, because it's not that important, and second, if it insists on getting in the way of your life and dreams, I'm going to find a way of kicking its ass myself, you hear me?"

I smile, and he puts his arm around my neck, squeezing me into an even tighter hug than before.

"I don't want you to think that every single thing that comes up in your life will make me stop being friends with you, dummy. I don't care how hard you try to stay silent, I'll insist until you tell me everything that's going on. Because you chose to be my friend and to tell me what's going on in your life, just like I tell you all the bad things that happen in mine, and that's not going to go away overnight."

His hands move toward my face, and his thumbs dry the tears under my eyes.

"Life is going to be different, Ian, but you can't stop living it. And I'm here for anything you might need, anytime you need it. Even if it's four a.m. on a Monday and you need to talk about how the moon is positioned in relation to all the stars in the universe. Just grab the phone and give me a call, because I'll always be ready to pick it up."

"Be careful what you wish for," I say, smiling in between tears. "When I start bugging you, you're going to regret those words."

"You can't bug me any more than you already do. I'll just have to endure it."

"Thanks, man" is all I can muster.

He smiles, and I reach for the door handle so I can go back home.

"What are you doing?" he asks.

"I think I'm . . . gonna go back home?"

"You made me drive all the way from Seropédica on a Thursday, and you think you're gonna get rid of me that easily?" He finally turns on the ignition, and the motor makes the tired sound of a machine that has been running way past its prime. "Close the door. We're going to Copacabana. I'm starving."

# CHAPTER 8

# VICTOR

THE TWINS LOOK LIKE THEY'VE been possessed by a horde of Tasmanian devils. They run from one corner of the living room to the other, fighting for the remote control, since Caíque wants to watch *Adventure Time* and Raí wants to watch a rerun of *Everybody Hates Chris*.

"You've already watched it a million times!"

"At least I understand what's going on in the story!"

"Mooooom, tell Raí to stop being such a brat!"

"Mooooom, Caíque won't let me have the remote!"

If you could hear them from a distance, you would think they were a pair of snot-nosed six-year-olds with their thumbs in their mouths. But no. Both are already twelve and continue to behave like overgrown babies.

"Victor, can you please find a way to deal with your brothers?" I hear my mom's voice from the kitchen, trying to project over their bellows and the imminent threat of a fight between the two of them as they start rolling on the floor over the remote.

"It wasn't *my* idea to take the Xbox and computer away from them!" I answer, knowing that if they weren't grounded, they'd be yelling at their *Overwatch* teammates on their headsets and blowing up heads left and right. Weirdly, when they interact with each other in the virtual world, they almost behave the way a normal person would expect of brothers.

"VICTOR!" my mother shouts, and I know that particular tone of voice means, "Don't you start your sass with me, you ungrateful boy, or you'll be next!" I roll my eyes, take a deep breath, and get up from the coffee table, where I was writing my review of *The Secret in Their Eyes* for my Latin American film class. I go to the outlet, squat, and with a mischievous smile, unplug the TV.

My brothers freeze, a tangle of skinny hands and feet and fresh scratches, stopping their fight to stare at me.

"Hey, this is between the two of us!" Caíque yells.

"Yeah, turn the TV back on, Victor!" Raí adds.

"So now you two have decided to become friends?"

"The enemy of my enemy . . ." Caíque doesn't finish the sentence.

"Okay, the two of you, for the love of God—*shut up!* I'm trying to study." I walk to the bookshelf and pick out two books, one by Stephen King and one by Dean Koontz. "Start reading these. I promise they're cool. Dead people and ghosts." I lower my voice, as if sharing a secret: "If you let me finish my homework, I'll let you use my computer after Mom goes to bed. I'll say you're in my room watching a movie. I'll even let you play your damn Xbox, but the volume will have to stay really low, and you can't say a word."

"You're gonna let us play all night?" asks Raí.

"Only till two, because if you don't wake up tomorrow, Mom will say it's my fault. Deal?"

They both consider it for a moment.

"Can we eat your cookies?" asks Raí.

"The ones in the pantry," adds Caíque.

"If you can keep quiet until Mom goes to bed, you can even eat the pantry door for all I care. Do we have a deal?" I ask.

The Tasmanian devils drop the books on the table and run to the kitchen, shoving each other to determine who'll get to open the cookies.

I try to focus on my homework, but my phone buzzes. Sandra is calling me, and I come to the conclusion that I'll never be able to finish this assignment, so I give up on trying. I grab my phone and plop down on the couch.

"So, what you up to?" she asks from the other end.

"Trying to stay sane while my brothers are deprived of their video games. And writing a paper."

"Are you done?"

"I have the words *This movie depicts*, but that's it."

"Wanna hang out?"

"Right now?"

"Yeah. I'm hungry, there's no food in the fridge, my parents went to the theater, and I'm utterly bored. Wanna come over?"

"My dad is working tonight, and my mom is by herself with the twins. I think she'd never forgive me if I went out right now. But you can stop by if you want."

"Okay."

She hangs up, and precisely five seconds later, I hear the doorbell.

That's the advantage of being best friends with your next-door neighbor.

+

"Any update on the 'Avoiding a boy I really like because I'm afraid to fall in love' soap opera?" Sandra asks once we're in my room, door locked. She's lying on my thigh as we both stare up at the ceiling.

She finishes eating a turkey-and-cheese sandwich she made for herself in the kitchen, and I toss a plush Bulbasaur doll into the air and catch it. My brothers finally calmed down and decided it would be a good idea to stop fighting, all for the privilege of playing video games late at night, and now they're sitting on the living room couch, watching the evening news and devouring chocolate cookies.

"Since when are you so interested in my love life?"

"Since it started happening, which is big news in itself. Come on, Victor, gimme some drama. My life is boring, and I can't stand watching TV shows anymore, so I need some *real* drama. Come oooooon!"

"You're such a cliché, you know that?"

"I am?"

"Yeah. If my life were a romantic comedy, you'd be the female character who's best friends with the lead. You're like a mix of the mentor and the comic relief, because I bet you have a lot of great advice to give, but you use none for your own life."

"In my movie," she retorts, "*you're* the trope, and this is the scene where the stereotypical gay best friend tells the main character about his love life, because he obviously has a funny voice, is full of little quirks, and even dyes his hair blue. We're all clichés, Victor."

"Whoa, now I'm offended. Which little quirks are these?"

"You just rolled your eyes," she said, even though she's still looking at the ceiling, not at me. "Am I right?"

Shit.

"Okay, we're all walking clichés."

"We're clichés within clichés, but now skip the script and start spilling the beans about the latest developments in your telenovela."

I remain silent.

"So . . ." I begin, and I notice Sandra is still quiet, waiting for my words. "Nothing has happened since I last updated you."

"What?!" She seems offended. "*Nothing?* Not one tiny thing? Not even a *hello* from him? Not even a poop or eggplant emoji?"

"Nothing. Absolutely nothing."

"It sounds like we have a problem that demands an immediate solution."

Before I realize what's happening, Sandra leaps from the bed and runs straight to my phone, grabbing it and unlocking the screen.

"Sandra, don't!" I say, because I know she's about to open my chat with Henrique and say something. That's what she always does, and sometimes I think it's funny, but right now I don't want her to.

My upset tone turns her fun smile to a serious expression. She locks the screen and gives the phone back to me, as if she were holding a bomb about to explode.

"Victor, I'll only say it again because we've been friends for a long time and I value our relationship: You like this Henrique guy in a way I've never seen you like anyone else, but you're letting your fear get the best of you."

"So what if I am?" All this talk of me having to give Henrique a shot despite everything else is starting to wear me out. "You're always talking about me being fearless, about believing in love and letting myself get into a relationship with a boy who might make me sick, but I doubt you'd do the same thing if you were in my shoes."

"If you really knew me, you'd know that would be the least of my concerns in a relationship. But apparently all these years have taught you nothing about me, and it seems I don't know the first thing about you, either. And HIV is not a sickness, you moron."

"So now you're the big relationship expert, are you?"

"Come on, Victor! Imagine what it must be like for *him* to like someone who also likes him but won't take another step forward because of something so minor. Where's the boy who came home all excited after finally going on a Tinder date with a normal person?"

"Something *minor*? If he'd told me about his status during the first date, maybe nothing would have happened. We probably wouldn't even be having this conversation right now."

"You have zero empathy, Victor. If you think this is hard for you, try putting yourself in his shoes for a moment, and think about what you would have done."

"Are you my friend or his? For God's sake, Sandra, put yourself in *my* shoes and think about what you would do!"

"I'd give it a try! My God, Victor, what are you so afraid of?! I remember you telling me the two of you had a really great connection and that you'd like to see him again. And after the second date, you were even more excited for the third. Dammit, Victor, he waited until the third date to kiss you! And you like him! Do you know what the odds are of finding someone you click with right away? Of having a date where you don't have to force conversation, where you want nothing more than to keep talking? Please, Victor, don't let fear loom over everything you two have. Henrique takes good care of himself, there's plenty of information out there, and it all agrees that a serodiscordant relationship can be as healthy as one between two negative people, if the two of you take precautions."

Sandra is being rational, but I don't want to hear anything she has to say. Maybe because she's expressing exactly what I've been thinking, and because she's using all her arguing power to disarm me.

Of course I was excited after the first date with Henrique, and not just because he was good-looking, with his copper hair that changes color under the sun, or the freckles that spread across his face, or his smile with slightly crooked teeth, or the awkward way he puts his hands in his pockets when he's feeling shy, shrugging a little.

All great points, but none count more than the conversations we had. We talked about the things we both enjoy (*Game of Thrones*, Harry Potter, *Sense8*—why, Netflix, why???—Hitchcock, Stephen King, *RuPaul's Drag Race*, and Diablo Cody), things we disagree about (he hates *The Lord of the Rings*, Woody Allen, and *Fringe*, while I hate *Lost*, *The Walking Dead*, and Björk), and things we both hate (Johnny Depp, Michael Bay, *Legends of Tomorrow*, and *The Secret*). We spent hours talking about movies and TV shows and directors, and he seemed interested when I started talking about cinematography, film editing, sound mixing, and other technical aspects of filmmaking besides screenwriting and acting. I paid attention when he talked about his job at the advertising firm, about his long hours in the office with pizza and Coke, and how he loves and hates all of it at the same time.

Next thing I knew, we were exchanging messages about a second date, and I couldn't stop thinking about him. When the day came, he showed up with a gift-wrapped package. I was so embarrassed for not having brought him anything, but he said I didn't have to worry about it. When I opened the box, I found an anniversary edition Blu-ray of *Pet Sematary*, probably my favorite horror movie of all time. Inside, a folded piece of paper said, *The greatest horror movie of all time*. My heart still jumps whenever I think about how I felt in that moment. I laughed and gave him a hug, thanking him, and he asked me to text him as soon as I was done watching it. He wanted to know if the Blu-ray edition was any different.

I started watching the movie as soon as I got home, maybe so I could spend a little more time with the Henrique that was starting to take form in my mind. I stared at his careful, round handwriting and was startled when the movie began.

It wasn't *Pet Sematary*, but *Transformers*. I laughed out loud when I reread the note. Yeah, this was definitely the greatest horror movie of all time.

And in that moment, I knew I had fallen for him.

But all that is behind us now. I'm not the guy with his head in the clouds from after our first, second, or third date. I am the guy who got into a relationship with someone who is HIV-positive, and I don't want that to define my life.

"I don't want to take precautions!" I rebut her last point, getting my thoughts back in order. "I don't want to spend my time thinking about all the things that could happen and about how I'm always at risk every time I kiss him!"

"You can*not* be serious!" Her eyes widen. "You know that kissing won't give you anything but herpes, right? Stop being such a hypocrite, Victor! When we go out, you're more than happy to make out with people whose names you don't even know, and now you're giving me this 'I'm gonna get HIV from a kiss' bullshit? I thought you were smarter than this."

Of course I know that, and I feel my ears burn for letting my prejudice get the best of me. I'm frustrated with this whole situation, and Sandra pressuring me only makes me more upset.

"Victor, I know you really like this guy." Her tone, subtle as a knife, makes me swallow. "When are you going to let go of this denial?"

"I'm not in denial!" I say, getting up from the bed. "I don't want to talk about this anymore, Sandra. I mean it. From now on, let's put this behind us and be done with it! He was a mistake, and there are plenty of fish in the sea."

"There are other people who may or may not be cool, who may or may not like you, who may or may not have HIV! And you *know* this guy is special. I've never seen you like this."

"I'm like this because I'm annoyed with this unnecessary conversation. Is your life really so boring that you need to insist on me getting a boyfriend?"

"I'll insist until you realize the best thing you can do is text him and tell him how you really feel."

"Oh, so that's what you want, is it?" I say, grabbing my phone and unlocking it.

I quickly remove his number from my contacts, then delete all our conversations.

"There, I deleted his number! Now there's zero chance I'll get in touch with him ever again!" I roar, throwing the phone on my bed.

"Why would you do that?" She seems shocked. "Undo it, Victor! Have you lost your mind?"

"I don't want to hear another word about this guy, Sandra. That's enough! It will never work, and I don't want to hear about it anymore. The end."

"You're going to regret this, and you know that."

"I started regretting it the moment I realized what I had gotten myself into. But now everything is back to normal."

"Great!"

"Great!"

She gets up from the bed, too, and she's clearly mad. "You're a judgmental moron, you know that, Victor?"

Without another word, she storms out of the room, slamming the door behind her.

I close my eyes at the bang and take a deep breath. I hear her opening the front door after saying a quick goodbye to Caíque and Raí, and then I see my mom's head poking into my bedroom.

"What happened?" she asks.

"Nothing," I respond impatiently. She just shrugs and leaves, knowing I'm not in the mood to talk.

Alone in my room, I sink into the bed and start thinking about what Sandra said. I grab my phone and check my messages, knowing that there's no way I can get Henrique's number back. But I also know that if he sends me a new message, I'll be able to see it.

I don't want to admit it—not even to myself—but I hope he will message me.

# CHAPTER 9

# HENRIQUE

WHEN I HAVE TOO MUCH on my mind, there's no better distraction than cleaning my apartment. I finished a project at work early, so they let me off, and I came back home, where the usual chaos of multicolored clothes was waiting for me.

Eric isn't home, so I take this opportunity to put on a Metallica album at maximum volume, then find a broom, some rags, and bleach to clean up all the mess in this house and to set my thoughts in order.

Organizing gives me a certain kind of power, as if arranging the objects on my nightstand by size were a way of sorting out my own life and all its chaos. Not that I'm complaining. Things are way better now than they were three years ago, when my parents were always around me, HIV was a scary novelty, and Carlos still professed his eternal love for me.

But it's not him I'm thinking about right now. Of course, Carlos still roams around my thoughts and, once in a while, makes a point of haunting me; I don't know if I'll ever be able to get over him. But at this moment I can only think about the two guys who came into my life recently and how they both claimed space inside me, each in his own way.

Victor is immature, but for some reason, he's the kind of person who makes me happy. The age gap between us isn't huge, but it feels like a wide chasm that I need to cross if I want to decipher all his fears. There's some alluring beauty in his awkwardness, in his dyed hair and preppy outfits, in how very slim he is and his preference for sad songs and strange movies. If things were different, I'd say he wasn't ready yet and try to convince myself he was just another disappointment and he wasn't worth it.

The problem is . . . I can't stop thinking about him.

At first, I thought it was because he uncovered my vulnerabilities and liked them—not the HIV, but in the other parts of my life. Not just that, he also exposed his own scars and anxieties about who he wanted to become in the future.

We didn't just talk about TV shows, movies, and music, but, thanks to all those things, we got along so well that it was easy to get into more intimate details. When I told him the story of how my mom had reacted to what she now refers to as my "life choice," Victor looked incredulous. He couldn't believe that she'd called being gay a perversion, that she had said there was no way she could respect someone as despicable as me, and that she couldn't even bring herself to imagine what people would say about her son and how he'd been raised, as if the conversation were about her and not about me. He went completely still as I told him about the weeks of silence, my frustrated attempts at reconnecting, and all the times I'd heard my mom cry, locked in her bedroom.

My *own* search for happiness was at stake, but it broke my heart to think I was hurting the most important person in my life like that. I told Victor I had tried to convince myself that it would pass, that in time my mother would talk to me again and look past the elephant in the room, but that didn't happen. The distance between us only increased as time went by, and she found new opportunities to hurt me with her unbearable comments, to the point where the only solution I could find was to fill my largest backpack with all the clothes I could fit and get the hell out of there.

And then, after I finished my story with the embarrassed smile of someone who has just delivered an unexciting conclusion, I asked Victor what it had been like for him to come out to his parents. He smiled, a bit shy, and said he had never had that conversation with them.

"They kind of know, you know?" Victor said, in that childish way of answering a question with a question. "Every time they talk to me about my love life, they ask about 'the boys.' The way I was raised was never too tied to the obligation of falling in love with someone of the opposite sex."

"Whoa" was all I could say. "You are so, so lucky."

"Yeah," he said with a smile. "I know."

It was always that way: Our conversations, dark as they were, always ended up with the two of us smiling like fools. Our dates left me with a good feeling, a sweet taste in the back of my throat that made me believe that I could in fact be happy and not consider it charity from the universe. Because HIV did that to me. Even after three years, it still has me believing that any amount of love I receive from another person is out of pity, that it isn't truly reciprocal.

But little by little, this worry is fading from my list of fears. I don't know how much Victor has to do with this change. I don't even know if he actually facilitated that process, or if my life adjusted and he just happened to be there, in the right place at the right time.

Here's what I do know: I like him, and I know he likes me, despite the combination of all these insecurities. And I'm tired of letting go of relationships that could be good out of a fear of rejection.

And that's where Ian comes in. This other guy, almost a fluke in my life, with whom I had a conversation that somehow made me reveal so much about myself and events that I hope will never happen again.

It's so strange how certain people seem to have an impact on your life all of a sudden and make you remember the things that happened to you and how you've evolved over time. Ian is me in the past, complete with all the anguish, uncertainties, fears. He's part of what I've been and of what I still am, and part of what is not worth going back to being.

The loud music and James Hetfield's deep voice are not enough to make me stop thinking about the two of them. The album is almost halfway through and the house has been officially turned upside down. Sweat trickles down my forehead, and my throat is dry from the effort of squatting to try and get to the places where the broom won't reach.

It's more or less then that Eric enters the room.

"YOU'RE THE WEIRDEST GAY MAN I'VE EVER MET!" he shouts above the music, scaring me half to death, and I whip my head around. My heart is beating fast, threatening to burst from my ribs. "FOR GOD'S SAKE, PLAY SOME BEYONCÉ!"

When I turn, I'm face-to-face with his six-foot-tall slender body wearing a handmade shirt that reads DADDY'S LIL MONSTER, orange-rimmed sunglasses, and braided hair hidden under a flat-brim hat with golden ornaments and a glitter dollar sign.

"You're cleaning up on a Friday afternoon? What's gotten into you?" Eric asks, throwing bags filled with shiny fabrics on the floor and sprawling on the couch.

I lower the volume and sit down next to him, sweaty and tired.

"I can't stop thinking about Victor."

"Still? Jeez, that guy really got in your head, huh?"

"I'm as surprised as you are."

"And what are you going to do about it?"

I shrug. "He's not interested."

"And you know that because . . . ?" He lets the question hang in the air.

"Because he stopped texting. Because he got scared and is probably thinking that dating an HIV-positive guy is too complicated."

"You're doing it again, Henrique."

"What?"

"Accepting it. Letting your fears get the best of you, letting them paralyze you."

"I don't do that."

"Of course you do. You pretend like you don't care because it's the easy way out. I know you."

"You know me, but I don't do that. He doesn't want this, so why should I insist?"

"Because you don't know that. What you *do* know is that he's scared, and I get that. You know what you need to do."

"I do?" I ask.

"Getting over your fear is the right choice. Allowing fear to get the best of you is also an option, but not the one I'd recommend. You can just drop it—of course you can—but there's a bit of advice that my mom used to give me, and I repeat it to myself almost every day."

"Hope for the best and expect the worst?"

He stares at me with a look of contempt. "It's better to suffer for something that you did than to suffer for what you didn't do."

"Was your mom a specialist in useless advice?"

"She baked cakes," he answers. "And she had to throw out many a dud when the recipe went wrong. But she'd never say, 'This recipe seems too complicated, so I won't even try.' She would just mix it all up and put it in the oven, and when it went wrong, she'd try again until she got it right."

"But the problem isn't getting something wrong. The problem is when the cake starts screaming, 'YOU GAVE ME A VIRUS! YOU DESTROYED MY LIFE!' Or when you start getting attached to the cake and it disappears without so much as a text, and next thing you know, the cake's getting all funny with a blackberry cheesecake."

"At least you got to eat the cake before it started screaming," Eric says with a devilish smile.

"You're the worst."

I lean my head on Eric's shoulder, and he doesn't mind that my hair is all sweaty from cleaning or that Hetfield's voice is still bellowing out of the speakers, though not as loudly as before.

"When did life become so complicated, my friend?" I ask him.

"When we decided we weren't happy enough being unicellular organisms, thought we'd start walking on earth, and evolved over billions of years to end up sitting on a couch, talking about relationships that won't move forward," he answers quickly, as if I asked an obvious question.

"Maybe."

"We make things more complicated than they are," Eric says. "Why don't you invite Victor to the party tomorrow? You'll get to talk, and he'll get to see Bibi Montenegro in her amazing Cleopatra performance!" Eric raises his arms in an exaggerated pose, chin jutting upward as if he expects a photographer from *Vogue* to show up at any moment.

"He won't answer."

"You're throwing out the ingredients before the cake even has a chance to bake," he answers, getting up from the couch and grabbing the bag of fabrics. "Well, your free therapy appointment is now over; I still have a lot of work to do. You've got a full living room to clean up, and don't go expecting my help with that. It's Friday afternoon, for God's sake!" he says, then heads toward his bedroom. He spreads the fabrics around the sewing machine and picks up the tin where he keeps the needles before closing the door. "AND PUT ON SOME BEYONCÉ!" he screams from the other side.

I change the music to "Formation," then look at the last two texts I sent to Victor, both unanswered.

I think to myself that this is stupid, but my conversation with Eric was, weirdly, very effective. So I type the name of the party, the address, the time, and how much tickets cost to Victor, and I press send. Then I copy the info and forward it to Ian, who could also use a distraction and might want to go out.

Both see the text almost right away. Ian sends me a thumbs-up and a wink emoji.

Victor doesn't respond.

# CHAPTER 10

# IAN

I GET HENRIQUE'S TEXT AS I'm waiting for the doctor at my appointment. I'm wondering if I should say yes or no, but the receptionist at the clinic calls my name, and all I can do is send two emojis before I get up and walk into the freezing office.

It's a small and somehow sad room. There's nothing but a poster on one wall, depicting two people—one is extremely thin and sickly looking, and the other has a perfect smile, tan skin, and a carefully trimmed beard—and underneath, the words HIV DOESN'T HAVE A FACE: A CARRIER CAN BE WHO YOU LEAST EXPECT. To the left, there's an exam table with a disposable cover on top of a thin mattress, an analog scale, and a sink, plus a small liquid soap container and a tissue dispenser drilled to the wall. To the right, the doctor's desk with two chairs in front of it extends from the wall across from the door to the other half of the room. There's a stethoscope on the table, a blood pressure monitor, a plastic pencil holder from Buenos Aires, and a beat-up book that, surprisingly, isn't medical, but a copy of *Howl* by Allen Ginsberg.

"Good afternoon, Mr."—she briefly glances at my chart—"Ian Gonçalves."

"Good afternoon, Dr. . . ." I let the sentence hang in the air.

She extends her hand and I shake it.

"Marcela Rodrigues."

I smile and sit in the chair across from her, leaving my backpack next to me.

She must notice me eyeing the book on her desk because she asks, "Are you a fan of beat poetry?"

"Actually, I only remember the opening verse of that poem. Usually I'm reading Dan Brown."

"He makes art history exciting." She smiles. "All literature is valid."

I smile, too, and in that moment I know she won't be a second version of the therapist who gave me my results.

I relax a little and let my shoulders drop, because the resemblance between her and the therapist is creepy. I felt my body tense as soon as I walked into the room and found another pair of cold blue eyes and blond hair, which this time was cut much shorter. I felt a brief panic, listening to her voice, because it is exactly the same as the therapist's, but her warm smile and the wrinkles on her face, which have clearly never gone under the knife, put me at ease.

"Do you by any chance have a sister?"

"At the clinic?" she asks. "Yes, but Teresa is older. Thirteen minutes. Which could mean bad luck, but actually just means I'm funnier, while she's the rude twin. No need to guess who is everyone's favorite, right?"

Her words come as a big relief, not only because they make it clear that I am with someone I can feel comfortable with but also because they put aside all my fears and insecurities, even if for only a few seconds.

"So, without further ado, let's see what we have here." She opens my file and reads the notes that the nurse scribbled when I talked to her. "Okay, Ian, aka six-four-three-eight: How are we doing today?" Her voice sounds optimistic and encouraging as she interlaces her fingers on the desk, watching me.

"Well, I think . . ."

"Right. Well. Well is good. Well is great. I need to ask some questions before I can explain to you how this process is going to work. I hope you'll be honest with me and won't take any of them personally, okay?"

"Okay."

"Do you use crack?"

"What?" I can't help but laugh at the question. *She's* the overly excited one who looks like she eats cocaine for breakfast, not me.

"Like I said, please don't be offended. And answer the questions. Are you a crack user?"

"No."

"Cocaine?"

"No."

"Marijuana?"

"Twice. Maybe three times in my life, I'm not totally sure."

"Cigarettes? Alcohol?"

"Tried the former and am sorry I can't quit the latter."

"Do you eat fruits and vegetables so they can turn into vitamins for your body?"

"Definitely."

"Chocolate? Starchy foods? Gluten? Lactose?"

"Yes, yes, yes, and yes."

"Perfect. Now, I want to know: Do you consider yourself to be a normal kid who now needs to take good care of himself because there's a virus in his bloodstream, or do you think HIV is a form of punishment that, I don't know, God or some higher power has something to do with?"

"Definitely option number one."

"So you don't believe in God?"

"I do; I just don't think He's so vengeful that He'd need to give me a virus so I could learn a lesson."

She smiles. "You're an interesting kid, Ian."

"I hope I won't offend you when I say . . . this is, without a doubt, the weirdest consultation I've ever had in my life."

"We've only known each other for three minutes, but I like to give my patients a good first impression. See this?" She grabs the pencil holder from the desk and lifts it up. "A patient gave it to me after a trip to Buenos Aires. And this?" She bends down and pulls out something wrapped in foil from her bag. "A slice of cake from another patient's fifteenth birthday party. I was actually at the

111

party last weekend, and he still insisted on bringing me more cake. Take note: My favorite patients are the ones who bring me cake."

"Why did you ask me all those questions? Are you making sure you don't need to call a social worker, or that I didn't get infected by needles?"

"Oh, needles! I forgot to ask about heroin. You don't use heroin, do you?"

"No."

"Great! I asked all those questions, Ian, because I can tell by your expression and the way you talk—and I'd hate to be wrong here—that you're the kind of guy who has already done some research on HIV ahead of time and that you have some basic understanding of it, too. Am I right?"

"Maybe you are."

"Of course I am. And at the risk of not upholding the oath I took as a doctor, I don't think we need to have that conversation about how saliva, sneezing, and hugs can't transmit HIV, correct?"

"Definitely."

"Great. Now I'd like to move on to the annoying routine that happens when you go to the doctor. So please have a seat on the exam table in the corner."

I obey, and in the next ten minutes, she checks my blood pressure (it's good), listens to my heartbeat (she nods), puts a tongue depressor on my tongue (she compliments my brushing and how straight my teeth are, thanks to the braces I had as a kid), asks me to cough, taps my stomach lightly, and listens to my breathing.

When she's finally satisfied, she goes back to her chair and asks me to return to mine.

"Seems like you're the healthiest person in this room, and I take pride in drinking green juice every morning!" She smiles encouragingly. "Now I want to focus on your exams." She points to a printed document and for the first time seems completely serious, which sends a slight chill up my spine. "This is your viral load count and the number of CD4 cells inside your body. You already know what CD4 cells are, right?"

"Yeah, they're defense cells."

"Perfect. The ideal number for a healthy individual is between five hundred and fifteen hundred cells per milliliter of blood. And this is your current count."

She turns the paper around so I can read the numbers she's pointing at.

396.

I feel my throat go dry. It's lower than the minimum amount.

"That's bad, right?" I ask.

"Not great, but also not terrible," she answers. "What you need to keep in mind is that this result is not by any means alarming. This other number"—she points to it—"is your viral load."

I look at the number and, surprised it's at all possible, feel my throat go even drier.

15,213.

"What do you know about viral load and CD4 cells in the body?" Dr. Rodrigues asks.

"I think I . . . didn't get to that point in my research," I answer, wiping the sweat off my hands. I have no idea how it's possible to sweat in a room like this, but I can feel my heart beating fast and my jagged breathing.

"Ian, try to calm down." She places a hand on my shoulder, and I know that's not something most doctors would dare to do, but the small gesture does me good. "Like I said, this is not a scary scenario. Your viral load might seem high, but you have nothing to worry about. The treatment brings it back to normal more quickly than you'd imagine."

I try to get my breathing under control and nod.

"Your CD4 count is a little under the ideal range, and the viral load, for someone who is still untreated, is under control. I've had patients here with three CD4 cells and a viral load of almost a hundred thousand, and the treatment still worked. So I want you to relax and try to stay positive. All right?"

"All right," I say, wondering if she told me this story to soothe me or if it really happened.

"Ideally, your CD4 goes up and your viral load goes down." She places her hands in front of her as if showing two levels. The left is lower to represent the viral load, and the right is higher to represent the CD4 cell count. "The first effect of the medication is to stop the virus from replicating inside your body. For us to achieve what we call an undetectable viral load, the number of copies per milli-liter of blood has to be below fifty."

"Fifty?" I ask, thinking about the over fifteen thousand I have now. "Down from fifteen thousand to fifty?"

"The medication brings that number down very quickly."

While she talks, Dr. Rodrigues writes frantically on a number of prescription pads, and I notice that her handwriting is true to the old medical chicken scratch stereotype.

"Well, here are a few exams you'll need to have done before the next appointment. It seems like a lot, and it is, but it's all just so I can make sure you're the healthy guy you seem to be. We have a blood test"—she hands me a piece of paper—"one for the kidneys and the liver"—another—"an echocardiogram"—and another—"a chest X-ray"—and another—"a test to detect if you've been exposed to tuberculosis"—and another—"and a simple urine and stool test." The last one, thank goodness. "Most of the exams you can take right here, and for the others, the receptionist can guide you to the nearest examination center."

"Jeez . . . This *is* a lot."

"No rush. Our next appointment"—she grabs a beat-up red notebook—"is in two months." She scribbles a date, asks what time works best for me, and then hands me a paper with all the details. "Now, let's discuss the dreaded antiretroviral cocktail. Are you ready?"

"One pill a day, right?" I ask.

"Darn it, did Fernanda tell you about them already?" she asks, referring to the nurse.

I smile.

"I'll give you a standard prescription for four months," she says, grabbing another piece of paper from the folder of endless sheets of paper, marking Xs in boxes, scribbling my name, and then stamping and signing it. "The pharmacy is on the second floor; you just go up the stairs and turn right. Hand this document to them, and they'll give you your bottle of pills. You can only get one per month, so you have to commit to coming here every single month." She drops the pen, interlaces her fingers again, and gives me a steady look, smiling. "And this is where I get a little less funny and become the responsible, serious doctor for a moment. My question is: Are you ready to make a commitment to this medication, Ian?"

"I am."

"These are not vitamins or cold medicine. This medication is not the kind you can forget to take for one day, or only do it for one week and then stop on Saturdays and Sundays. You know that, don't you?"

I nod.

"And do you know why it is that you can't stop taking it for even one single day?"

"Not exactly, but I know it has to do with the virus mutating inside my body. Am I right?"

"You're more curious than I thought. That's exactly right." She grabs a white piece of paper and starts drawing. To the left, she draws a diamond shape with a line inside it, and underneath, several identical shapes. To the right, she draws a square, a circle, a triangle, and a pentagon, all of them with different lines inside. "Imagine that on the left we have a flu virus. It multiplies quickly, but its mutation happens over a long period of time. If you don't take the medicine, the virus continues to multiply in your body, and then when you take it again, the medication continues to be efficacious, because it was manufactured to eliminate that specific mutation that it identified in your body." She circles the different shapes now. "With HIV, though, it's a different scenario. While it takes a long time to destroy your defense cells, its mutation happens very quickly. It's as if the flu virus multiplied itself on a photocopy machine, and HIV multiplied itself based on drawings made by a toddler. The copies aren't identical, so even two days without the medicine running through your bloodstream makes it unable to identify the new copies and greatly narrows our medicine options. There are several different combinations, but it's important for us to try not to burn through all of them unless absolutely necessary."

"Right. And are the side effects really awful?"

"A little at first, I'm afraid," she says. "One of the composites of the three-in-one drug alters the nervous system a bit, and the effects can be similar to symptoms of depression, as well as nightmares and anxiety. But it only seems bad, and I promise you that things get better with time. That's why one of the recommendations is that patients take the medicine at a specific time—before bed, for instance—to minimize side effects. If you think you can't deal with them, which is perfectly understandable, we can change the treatment option. But for now, I'd like you to use it, since it's the most widely offered medication in the pharmacy. Okay?"

"Okay."

"Now, remember when I asked you about drugs and gluten? Do you think certain habits meddle with the medication's efficacy?"

"I wouldn't know how to answer this one."

"Nothing, absolutely nothing, can stop this medication. Not crack, not cocaine, not alcohol. Which means that, as much as I strongly advise you not to try hard drugs and especially injectable drugs, you *could* use them without affecting your treatment. You just need to be responsible, whether it's a joint or a beer. Are we clear?"

"Perfectly."

"The question about God was important, too, because some people stop treatment if they believe in a miracle cure, and they come back with higher and higher viral loads. I hope you are not one of those people."

"I won't be."

"Great. The goal of treatment, Ian, is to reach an undetectable viral load of fewer than fifty copies. When HIV is undetectable in your body, it becomes negligible. It's not a proper cure, because if you stop taking the meds, the virus goes back to multiplying inside your body, but it's the closest we can get to having control over it. When you become undetectable, your chances of transmitting HIV to someone are effectively zero. It's imperative to follow treatment to the letter, not only for your own health but for the health of others, understand?"

"Absolutely."

"I also want to draw your attention to PrEP. Have you heard of PrEP?"

"I don't think so."

"PrEP stands for pre-exposure prophylaxis. It's a little blue pill that those who are HIV-negative can take once a day to dramatically decrease their chances of contracting the virus. So, if you were to have a partner who is HIV-negative and on PrEP, and you're undetectable and following proper treatment, then there would be effectively zero chance of transmitting the virus to your partner. In fact, proper treatment and PrEP are the most effective ways to reduce acquisition of HIV among men who have sex with men."

"That's really good to know."

"Still, this isn't to say that you should have sex without a condom. If you don't use them, you could run the risk of being re-infected with a different strain of HIV by someone who is also positive. And nobody wants that, right?"

"Once was bad enough."

"Yes, we don't want treatment to become more complicated. So we're on the same page, then. I'll schedule another appointment for next week just in case you think the side effects of the medicine are intolerable, but I believe it will be a piece of cake for you. If you are doing okay with the medicine, I'll look forward to seeing you in a couple of months with the tests I ordered so we can track how the medicine is working in your body. Deal?"

"Deal."

We shake hands. Hers is thin, bony, and cold, but soothing.

"I hope this is the start of a good relationship from here on out, Ian. I know it's kind of a cliché thing to say, but if you commit to the treatment, your life can be perfectly normal. It's not an insurmountable task, as you can see, and I'm sure your treatment will be a success."

I smile, and for the first time since HIV showed up in my life, I feel a little more optimistic about the future.

# CHAPTER 11

# VICTOR

I DECIDE TO GO FOR a drink with a crew from school. Like most groups of assorted individuals that can be called a crew, mine consists of seven or eight itinerants who can each be substituted without notice by someone else, depending on who has class on any given day.

It's a loud group filled with different ideas and perspectives, and in a group of film majors that means a lot of multicolored hair, secondhand clothing, Frida Kahlo bags, and Moleskine notebooks, which we use to write down witty one-liners that can later be used in scripts. The crew spends more time arguing about the problems of the world than actually doing anything to solve them, with conversations fueled by cold beer and greasy appetizers from dive bars around Cantareira.

I still haven't made up with Sandra since our argument, so maybe that's why she left an empty chair between us when she sat down, which we proceeded to fill with all the bags that the crew lugs around for classes.

We begin with our vices. Cigarettes, cell phones, and glasses full of beer are essential in these gatherings, and I'm no exception. My eyes are glued to Henrique's last message, giving me the place and time for a party tomorrow. I'm still unsure if I should go, if I should say I'm going and then not show up, or if I should just ignore him.

"There's this dancer who everyone thinks is HIV-positive," I hear one of the girls tell a guy, and my attention is drawn from my phone to their conversation when I hear that word, as if some alarm has gone off inside me. "So no one wants to dance with him, too afraid of getting infected by his sweat and such. It takes place in San Francisco in the 1980s."

"What?" I ask, and I notice Sandra looking over at me with curiosity.

"*Test.* A movie I saw yesterday about the beginning of the AIDS epidemic and how everyone called it the gay virus. The main characters are in a dance company, and there are some really beautiful scenes with their choreographies. There's also a really great sentence that I wrote down here." She pulls out her Moleskine, turning the pages full of sketches and incomplete scribbles until she finds what she's looking for. "'Fuck art. Let's dance.' This is what one of the characters tells the other in the middle of the movie. I thought it was really beautiful."

"Fuck art?" one of the guys asks. "We make a living from art, Erica. That's a little offensive, no?"

"No, no. In the context of the movie, it makes a lot of sense. It's like, 'Let's stop analyzing the things that might not even mean that much after all and be free,' or 'Let's live, we've got our whole lives ahead of us,' you know? At least that's how I read it."

"It's really wild how quickly things escalated, isn't it?" another guy interjects, one with an anemic look about him and who seems to feed exclusively on Proust. "Overnight, everyone started dying, and no one knew what it was, just that the only ones dying were gay. It must have been terrifying."

"I think it's still terrifying, actually," says the girl who saw the movie, putting away her Moleskine. "We still haven't eradicated AIDS in the world."

"Oh, of course not. But these days things are under control . . ." The guy loses his train of thought. "What I mean is, it's treatable, so you can live relatively well with someone who has HIV."

"You're just saying that." I notice Sandra joins the conversation nonchalantly, but I look at her cautiously. She stares at me with a determined look.

"And you seem quick to judge someone just by what they say." The guy seems offended. "It's as if we're saying that, I don't know, we can't or shouldn't date people with HIV."

"Would *you* date someone who is HIV-positive?" Sandra asks without a second thought, staring at the guy as if challenging him. She darts her eyes at me again for a millisecond, and I know it's meant as a provocative question.

"Why not?" he answers, shrugging. "I think nowadays positive people can live just fine with the virus. If they took good care of themselves and we used condoms, I don't see why that would be a problem."

"Ugh, no, y'all, that'd be super complicated," a girl named Luana chimes in, speaking for the first time before she takes a gulp from her beer. "Easier said than done. You can't just dive into a relationship like that without acknowledging that it's a risk."

"But isn't *every* relationship a risk?" Sandra asks, looking at Luana. "Or do you require blood tests from everyone you have sex with?"

"No! It's one thing to use a condom for a casual hookup, but something else entirely to commit to using them for the rest of your life!"

"It's all about condoms, then? Even if you're in love with the person and they might be the love of your life? You're giving a lot of power to a piece of latex."

"So you'd be in a relationship with someone who had HIV?" asks Luana, crossing her arms, clearly annoyed at the point Sandra's making.

"Yes! I don't know, I don't even think I'd mind, if the person took good care of themselves."

"You're only saying that because you've never been in that situation," I blurt out, and I regret it almost immediately, because she shoots daggers at me with her eyes. Suddenly, all eyes are on me.

I swallow, and when everyone remains silent, I go on: "It's easy to say, 'Yeah, I'd get into a relationship with someone who's positive, no worries!' when you're not in that situation. Once you're in that situation, everything gets more complicated."

Me and my big mouth.

"Have you been in a relationship with someone you knew was positive, Victor?" Luana asks.

Before I can answer, Sandra interrupts, "Whoa, Luana, rude much?"

"What?" The girl seems confused.

"I don't think that's anyone's business."

"We're all friends here, Sandra" is her attempt at explaining herself.

"Still. Rude."

"I'm sorry." Luana raises her hands to indicate that she's innocent. "No need to answer that if you don't want to, Victor."

"I haven't been in a relationship yet with someone who has HIV, at least not to my knowledge," I answer, offending Sandra even more with my lie. "But I've talked to someone who's on treatment, and he seemed more shaken psychologically than physically."

"And assuming you were interested in that person, knowing that he's positive, would you take the next step? Like, would you continue to show interest?" asks Luana.

"As a reminder, this is potentially the love of your life, and the two of you could be happy forever, and all this relationship needs to work is an ultra-thin piece of latex and some doctor's appointments," adds Sandra. "Is that too high a price to pay for happiness?"

The conversation is getting more uncomfortable by the second, and I'm sure Sandra is doing this on purpose. Not that she brought up the subject, but she certainly sustained it to the point that it became the main topic of discussion.

I feel my ears burning when I notice that all the other conversations around the table have died down, and everyone is watching me, waiting for my answer. I start considering the possibility of offering a politically correct "Yes, I would." At the same time, I also think about saying that this is stupid and there are too many people in the world for me to end up getting involved with somebody who could make my life more complicated.

"I don't . . . know," I respond, and that's all I can say.

At the moment, it's the truth.

Dammit, I'm so confused. I can't stop thinking about Henrique and Ian, can't stop thinking about all the fears and frustrations of living with HIV. I can't stop imagining myself in their shoes, hearing awful things every single day in casual conversations like this one.

I'm mad at myself because I start thinking about who I was before I met them and how I thought people who got infected with STIs deserved it because they had been stupid enough not to be more careful. Because they'd been promiscuous. Because they'd let themselves get into situations that could have easily been avoided.

But the problem is that neither Henrique nor Ian will get second chances, and it's hypocritical to think I'm better than they are when I don't even know what kind of sex life each of them leads or has led. For all I know, I might have had many more sex partners than Ian or Henrique, so who am I to judge what happened to them?

I'm mad at myself when I think of how stupid I was for judging people I barely even knew.

"'I don't know' is what separates us from our own happiness, Victor." Sandra looks me straight in the eye for the first time today, and I feel a wave of relief wash over me when I realize she's talking to me, even if not in a friendly way. "Don't be the 'I don't know' guy."

I swallow my beer and flash a sheepish smile at what it seems to mean: end of discussion. I cough and say I need to go to the bathroom, trying to draw attention away from my flushed cheeks and sweaty forehead.

I walk into the filthy bar and wash my face in the sink outside the men's bathroom. I try to take a deep breath with my eyes closed, ignoring the music from the jukebox and the loud laughter from the people playing pool.

"That was a little hypocritical of you." I hear Sandra's voice behind me.

I dry my face with my forearms and rub my eyes, trying to piece my thoughts back together.

"What do you want from me, Sandra?" I ask, weary.

"I don't want anything. But what about you, Victor? What do *you* want?"

"I already told you . . . I don't know."

"Of course you do. I know you know, and more important, *you* know you know. You just need to admit what it is you really want and leave your fears behind you."

I feel my eyes sting.

Dammit.

"You're right, okay? You're right and I'm wrong and I got desperate because it's something I don't know about and it's been terrifying me ever since it appeared in my life." Before I can catch myself, I'm spilling it all out and can't stop. "I don't have the slightest idea how to deal with this or how to stop thinking about it twenty-four seven, Sandra, and I might have been a jerk, but you know what? I'm really fucking confused. I can't stop thinking about that idiot and all the things he's been through in his life. I can't lie down at night without his name running around in my head and that stupid face appearing before me every two minutes. So, yeah, I might have been a jerk, but I don't want to be one anymore! He texted me after I deleted his number and invited me to a party tomorrow, and I didn't know if I'd go or not, but I just decided that I will, because I can't stop thinking about him! And I hate that you didn't know that he texted me and invited me to a party, because if you had known, you would probably have already insisted that I go and this wouldn't be eating me from the inside out. So, for God's sake, I don't want to fight anymore!"

And then, out of nowhere, the tears start coming. Right there in the middle of the bar, surrounded by loud music, the smell of urine, and the noise of pool balls hitting one another, my eyes swell with tears, my breath becomes ragged, and the air doesn't flow into my lungs as easily. I'm sure that the beer I drank this afternoon has something to do with this sudden burst of emotion.

Sandra hugs me, and a hug is all I need right now.

I try to control my breath while I bury my head in her shoulder, feeling my heart pulse wildly in my chest to the beat of a name.

Hen. Ri. Que. Hen.

Ri. Que. Hen. Ri.

Que. Hen. Ri. Que.

# CHAPTER 12

# HENRIQUE

MY APARTMENT LOOKS LIKE AN episode of *RuPaul's Drag Race*.

Whenever there's a performance scheduled, the drag queens who live too far from downtown meet up at a house closer to the bar to get ready for the show, and today it's Eric's turn to host.

The apartment is a confusing mess of multicolored tissues and garments. Various shades of gold, silver, and blue are spread around the floor and chairs, every inch of the dining room has been taken over by makeup, and the bedroom mirror has somehow ended up in the living room, where the single painting we own used to hang on the wall. I have to admit, I might just keep it there.

Everyone is lined up in front of the mirror, all shirtless, with pieces of tape stuck to their foreheads to hold their hair as they transform their sharp, masculine faces into softer features, eyes lined with makeup and full lips covered in a thousand different colors of lipstick.

"So, Henrique . . ." One of the girls looks at me through the reflection in the mirror. (When they're all together, they refer to one another with female pronouns and their drag names, which is both funny and welcoming.) "Bibi told me you're seeing a new boy. Tell us about him!"

Bibi Montenegro is Eric's stage name. They all have names they chose themselves or that were chosen by close friends: Maicon, Felipe, and Tulio are now Mad Madonna, Kara Parker, and Nicolle Lopez, respectively. Each one has an explanation ready as to why they were christened with that drag name. (In Eric's case, it's an homage to his favorite actresses, Bibi Ferreira and Fernanda Montenegro.)

"I'm not seeing anyone new," I say right away, looking at Bibi, who raises an eyebrow in total twenties femme fatale fashion, then gives me a sideways smile. "Bibi talks too much."

"If you hadn't gone so red so quickly, I'd say Bibi was the biggest liar of the group. But in this case, I think she might be telling the truth," Mad Madonna retorts, closing one eye to apply eye shadow. "Spit it out, girl! We've never had secrets between us, and you've always been so reserved and . . . single! This calls for a celebration!"

"I heard Henrique invited the boy to the party tonight," Bibi mumbles in a fake whisper that everyone can hear.

The squeals start immediately.

Great, now all eyes are on me.

"Come on, Henrique, what's he like?! Is he tall? Strong? Thin? Does he have a little meat on his bones?" Kara Parker asks. "Give us a clue!"

I glare at Bibi, unhappy, but she just gives me a cynical wink and puts on a thick black wig, adjusting the strands with her fingertips.

"Okay, but do you swear—*really* swear—that you'll leave him alone if he shows up tonight?"

"For Judy Garland's sake and the love of Liza Minnelli, I swear," Mad Madonna says, raising one hand.

"For Judy Garland's sake and the love of Liza Minnelli, I swear," they all repeat, including Bibi.

"Great." I pull out my phone and search for a photo of Victor, then show it to everyone.

"Oh, he's so young!"

"And thin!"

"With blue hair! A rebel, I like it!"

"What's his star sign?"

"Does he have a tattoo?"

"Is he still breastfeeding? He must be, like, twelve."

"Enough!" I grab the phone back, and they all start laughing. "Are you bitches happy now?"

"Of course not!" Nicolle Lopez says. She puts on a gold choker and adds an accessory to her wig, a gold chain that dangles down to her forehead with a jewel that looks like an emerald. "We'll only be satisfied when he's here snuggling with you and you're calling each other cute stupid names, like sweetheart and sweetie."

"Shaaade!" Kara Parker yells, looking over at Mad Madonna as they all start laughing. *Sweetheart* and *sweetie* are what Mad Madonna and her boyfriend call each other.

"Girl, I'd rather sound ridiculous calling my sweetie *sweetie* than have to come up with a cute nickname because I don't actually know the name of the guy I'm hooking up with at any given moment."

"I can't help it if I have short-term memory loss," Kara Parker shoots back with a smile. "Hi, who are you again?"

"Your worst nightmare!"

"That seems about right with that makeup job of yours."

And that's how the evening progresses—a constant exchange of insults that makes everyone laugh out loud.

"Girls, focus!" Bibi announces after about fifteen minutes of gossip and little skirmishes among the queens. Her face is all done, and she walks from one side of the room to the other, just waiting for the queens to wrap up before putting on her long blue dress. "Our friend is finally getting out of his shell, and that is reason for celebration!"

She runs to the kitchen while everyone claps, then comes back with a giant box of wine.

"Where did you get that from, Bibi?" I ask, my eyes wide at how huge it is.

"I have secret places you wouldn't believe," she answers, winking again, and everyone laughs one more time.

Bibi grabs some disposable cups from the kitchen and places them in a spot that's not covered in makeup and fabrics, then starts pouring the cheap wine.

"Girl, if you stain my dress with wine, I'll kill you, cast a spell to bring you back, and then kill you all over again!" Nicolle grumbles, pulling her dress away from the table as Bibi hands each of the girls a cup.

"I can't believe you're toasting to me getting out of my shell, which by the way, hasn't happened yet," I say with a smile, because it's impossible to stay sad when all these wonderful people come together to whip out catty remarks.

"I'm an incurable optimist, darling," Bibi says, raising her cup. "A toast to being who we are, with all our faults and issues!"

"A toast to Adore Delano!"

"A toast to Sarah Jessica Parker!"

"A toast to Madonna!"

"A toast to us!" I say, because right now, that's all I can think of being thankful for.

I down the wine in one gulp and feel the liquid scratch my throat.

"Holy crap, this wine sucks, doesn't it?" Mad Madonna complains, coughing after she swallows it. And yet she grabs the box and pours herself another cup. "Why would you ruin our cute moment with this vinegar, Bibi?"

+

I think I had more wine than I should have.

I definitely had more wine than I should have.

The big disadvantage of having the queens over and helping them get ready for the show is that they always drink too much, but they somehow manage to maintain their shine and composure. Unlike me, who sees two of everything and feels all the liquid dancing in his belly, not to mention has an urgent need to pee.

Or maybe I got too excited and everyone else knew when to stop.

Yeah, that must be what happened.

We call two taxis for the group from a company we all know and trust. As much as I hate to admit it, a news story starting with "Four drag queens and a drunk guy got into an unregistered cab" doesn't always end well these days, and even though our place isn't far from the club, wandering the streets of Rio at night with four tipsy friends isn't exactly safe. But now we're off to the club, and the world keeps turning.

The taxi driver welcomes us with a grin and kisses on the cheeks, asking us how we're doing and saying that, unfortunately, he can't make it to the show tonight. Kara Parker says she'll give him tickets for free and hugs him, but the driver says his boyfriend wouldn't like that, which makes her step away with an unhappy look on her face.

When we get there, the line to get in hasn't formed yet, but there are a good number of people at the entrance, smiling, holding cups full of cheap wine and beer. Inside, multicolored lights are flashing, and the front door lets out some of the music that the acoustic walls try to muffle. Some panhandlers try to start conversations with people while hawkers try to make a quick buck selling gum, candy, and cigarettes.

Bibi steps out of the car like a Hollywood star about to walk the red carpet. She holds both sides of her long dress and pulls them up to keep the dress from brushing the ground, revealing her gold sandals, but her body is covered with a coat so the dress won't be seen ahead of time. People start looking right away, and she smiles. She loves being the center of attention, especially tonight, when she's the main attraction.

I look around and step back when I notice some people walking toward her to ask for autographs and pictures. Bibi is a bit of a celebrity on drag nights, which always scores her and her friends some free booze. I check my phone and notice my battery is about to die, since I forgot to recharge it.

"Henrique!" I hear Bibi calling to me between the camera flashes and Instagram videos. "Are you all right?"

I think she and everyone else has noticed that my alcohol level is a bit above average, but it's nothing I can't handle.

"Sure!" I answer maybe a little too excitedly. "Everything is wonderful!"

She realizes I'm splitting my attention between my phone (the battery has gone down) and looking around me in hopes of finding Victor's blue hair and thin face, but she doesn't say anything. I appreciate it when Bibi is discreet, especially because I know it's a rare occurrence.

"I'm going to the dressing room, my friend. If you need me"— she leads me to the entrance and points at a five-foot-tall girl, the tips of her hair dyed green, who smiles at everyone as she hands out a few VIP wristbands—"Rebecca will show you how to get there."

Bibi hands me a band and adjusts it around my wrist.

"My God, Henrique, you're such a stranger!" Rebecca says, pulling me in for a hug.

"Rebeccaaaaaa," I say, hugging her. "I looove you!"

"Oh, gosh, you're drunk."

I shrug. "Maybe I am, if you think half a gallon of cheap wine is enough to get someone drunk." My smile widens, my eyes narrow, and Bibi rolls hers and ignores me. "But not enough to be embarrassing, because today is the day of our star, Bibi! I don't want to be responsible for throwing up in the middle of the crowd and ruining her night."

"Very wise, Henrique." Bibi kisses my cheeks and then whispers to Rebecca, "Take care of him, will you? Text me if anything happens."

"You got it, Bibi," answers Rebecca. "You can go in whenever you're ready, Henrique."

"Yes, ma'am!" I say when I see Bibi disappear in the club's lights. "In a moment! I just need some"—I point to the vendor stalls—"some tequila!"

I turn my back to her, stumbling, and bump into Mad Madonna, who steadies me and stops herself from cursing when she recognizes who it is. I kiss her hand to make up for it, then move forward in my search for more alcohol.

I don't know why I decided it was a good idea to get drunk

tonight of all nights. What I do know is that there's little thinking involved once you start drinking, because all your stupid ideas suddenly seem great, and the booze going down your throat doesn't sting as bad.

I breathe out through my mouth and order a shot of tequila from a woman who screams, "Three for ten!" and "We take credit cards!" I say yes, because I'm in no condition to do the math. She places three disposable cups on top of the Styrofoam container where she keeps the liquor, then hands me slices of lime and a packet of salt. I place the salt on the back of my hand, lick it, and down the three shots of tequila before sucking on the lime, which somehow tastes sweeter than the drink.

Yeah, I guess I wasn't right when I said the booze stops stinging as bad after a while.

Still grimacing, I order a bottle of beer to wash away the sourness of the lime. I grab my wallet and pay her without bothering to check if the change she gave me is correct.

I walk away, heading toward the stairs of a building near the entrance to the club, where a few people are sitting and talking. I find a corner for myself, put the beer bottle between my legs, and take the phone from my pocket again.

Why is it that every stupid idea seems great when you're drunk?

My fingers find the messenger app automatically, where I check the last message I sent Victor, with the name of the club and time of the party. Suddenly, my feelings go from complete apathy to intense rage. It's as if I've had an epiphany: Victor is being childish and ghosting me. Screw his fears and all the things he's feeling. I'm tired of being the person who always needs to offer more than the other one is willing to give me. I'm tired of HIV being the main character in my relationships, and I'm tired of thinking I owe a sentimental debt to others. Fuck all of it and everyone!

My movements are automatic: The bottle of beer going back and forth between my legs and my mouth, only half its cold contents flowing down my throat; a held-back burp that makes my eyes sting and my breath catch; my thumb pressing the button to record a voice message to Victor, the phone coming closer to my mouth; and now me speaking.

"I thought you were different, Victor." I feel my diaphragm rising suddenly with a hiccup. I cough, then keep talking. "But you're just like everyone else. Just like Carlos. I thought we'd have a chance at being happy. You think it's cool that I like you so much and I can't be with you because of this crap? Because of your fear and your selfishness, when I know you like me, too? Because I know, man, even if you want to deny it: I saw it in your eyes. You're scared, and I swear I tried to take that into account, but you know what? Fuck it! Fuck you and your fears. What about *my* fears? *My* selfishness? Do you think it's easy for me to wake up every day and not think about this fucking virus? Because I think about it every day; it's the first thing on my mind when I wake up and the last I think about when I go to sleep. Maybe it is my true love, because it's with me twenty-four hours a day, even after three years. I tell myself everything is okay, that I shouldn't be thinking about it, but it's the same as telling someone who's hungry that they shouldn't focus on being hungry, that it'll go away soon. It's inevitable. Because I know I have a right to be happy, but it's so . . . so . . . *frustrating* to know that happiness is so close and this virus is a force field that doesn't let me take another step forward." I take a deep breath, trying to keep another hiccup at bay. "And that's what I mean: I want to be happy, but I'm tired of begging for it. If you don't want to set your prejudices aside, great, be happy with them. I'll try to be happy as best I can, and when I make it, I want to look in your face and laugh. You know why? Because I'll be happy, and you won't make me miserable with your selfishness."

I let go of the record button and stare at the little bubble, the word *delivered* appearing underneath it. I'm satisfied with my speech. Victor needs to hear it, since he won't show his face or answer my texts anymore. It's the least he should know.

I drink the last of my beer and try to get up way too quickly, tripping on myself and being helped by two female hands.

"Whoa, careful there, buddy!" It's a short girl, looking at me with mild annoyance. When she gets to my face, though, her expression changes, and she grins. "Hey! It's you!"

I take a step back and rub my eyes, frowning and staring at her. I don't know this girl. She must be one of Bibi's fans who saw me in a picture with her.

"Sorry, but . . . do I know you?"

"Oh, you don't know me, but I know you!" She smiles triumphantly. "Very nice to meet you. My name is Sandra, and I'm here with a friend who knows you very well. Victor, look who I found!"

I look back and see the blue-haired boy grabbing two beers

from the woman who just sold me the three tequila shots.

He smirks, and at the same time I stare at my phone screen.

The voice message went through, and then the screen goes dark as my battery dies.

Shit.

# CHAPTER 13

# IAN

IT'S A GIANT WHITE PILL, the size of an antibiotic for strep.

I look at it in the light, turning it around in my fingers. Wouldn't it be ironic if it got stuck sideways in my throat and I choked to death? Maybe not—definitely not—but I can't stop thinking about the possibility and laughing morbidly at my reflection in the bedroom mirror.

I'm ready for the party, and the Uber is on its way, but I continue to stare at the pill and wonder if it's a good idea to take it tonight, right as I'm about to go out by myself to meet people I don't know very well. I wonder if it might make me melancholy or something, because the side effects include dizziness, negative thoughts, and nightmares. Nothing in there about hallucinations, so seeing a black-winged monster flying around the club shouldn't be on my list of fears, but I still can't help but think that right now might not be the best time to start the medication.

But I also consider that it might be a good idea to take the first pill now, on a night when I won't go straight to sleep. It might make my body send a message to the meds, like, "Hey, I don't want to have nightmares!" or something. It also seems like a good idea to take it when I know I'll drink and get dizzy from the alcohol anyway.

I'm tired of weighing the outcomes in my head, so I just shove the pill into my mouth and go to the kitchen to find a glass of water. I take a long gulp and force the pill down to my stomach.

Toward the virus.

+

I'm not used to going out in Rio de Janeiro at night. I'd much rather stay in bed watching a show or reading a book, even though everyone tells me it's an antisocial thing to do and that I'll end up alone surrounded by cats and books. It's comfortable, fun, peaceful, and quiet. But today I don't want quiet, because I know it would drive me wild. It would make me think about things I don't want to think about, make me brood over the past and become sad, and I don't want to go through that tonight, not now that the meds can amplify my feelings.

The car snakes through the streets toward downtown Rio. The driver asks me if I want any candy, if the temperature is okay, and if I want to listen to any particular radio station. My curt replies stop him from trying to make more small talk, which makes me less annoyed with his previous attempts. I stare out the window, watching the lights pass quickly by my eyes.

I get out of the car and head to the club, certain it will be a good night out. Maybe I won't find either of the guys, but I still think it'll be fun to see the drag queens performing onstage. I've never been to this club before, but based on the ads Henrique sent me and his own reviews of the songs they play here, I'm sure I'll have a great time.

The first thing I notice is that this is definitely not the kind of club the guys from my economics class drag me to every once in a while. All the colorful hair, baggy clothes, and glitter assure me that this is a different kind of place. I see tall women, and it takes me a moment to realize they're men wearing makeup; I see boys hugging other boys and girls hugging other girls, and I can't find anyone judging them, not even the panhandlers outside or the vendors in the booths near the entrance.

There's a small line to get in, bouncers checking IDs, and people drinking and smoking. Some of them take photos with drag queens, who smile, sneer, and throw out catchphrases.

I take out my phone and text Henrique to let him know I'm here. I know he invited me, but I don't know if he's already here. I look around, searching for familiar faces, but find none. I shrug and turn to one of the ladies in a booth to get a beer, and I can feel that my senses are more acute. I think the first of the side effects is starting to show—in this case, dizziness.

I lean against a wall, take a sip of the beer, and close my eyes, trying to force things back to their rightful places. It's as if someone pressed the fast-forward button on a movie and everything has started happening way too quickly. I feel the sole of my foot getting warm, and a heat that's not actual heat takes over my body. I feel hot, but I'm not sweating. It's a bizarre feeling, at the same time bothersome and bearable.

Maybe it wasn't a good idea to take the pill before going out, but I don't want to go back home. I take a deep breath, look ahead of me, and stare at the people speeding by, laughing without a care in the world. I start wondering if any of them are faking it, like I am, pretending everything is all right. If they are laughing just out of peer pressure, because it's easier than locking yourself up in your bedroom to worry over the bad stuff.

I look at my phone and see Henrique hasn't replied. I shrug, finish my beer, and decide to get in line. I hear a Lady Gaga song playing and everyone singing along. Still a bit dizzy, I lean on a barricade so I won't stumble into anybody, then pay for my ticket and go inside.

It's as if I've entered a psychedelic dream full of strobe lights. The floor vibrates with the bass, and people walk in every direction in search of alcohol, the bathroom, or friends. A DJ is onstage wearing headphones, his hands swift on the sound board, mixing and making the transition from one track to the next. When he changes the song, everyone yells excitedly and starts singing along.

It occurs to me that it's going to be a little hard to find Henrique in this big place with all these people, but the moment I see three people dancing under a staircase, I immediately recognize Victor's blue hair and startling height, as well as Henrique's red hair and pale skin; next to them is a girl wearing a black outfit with a red ribbon in her hair.

"HI!" I scream over the music, and Henrique flashes a smile at the sight of me. He gives me a hug, and I feel his body propping itself against mine, which leads me to believe he's already drunk. I wave to Victor when Henrique lets go, and he hugs me. The girl I haven't met waves shyly, but when she realizes I'm with the group, she hugs me, too.

Everyone smells great, even Henrique, even after his cologne got mixed with sweat and the alcohol I can smell on his breath.

"IAN!" Henrique bellows. "THIS IS SANDRA, AND I GUESS YOU'VE ALREADY MET VICTOR!"

Before I can get used to the loud music or make any sort of comment about the red ribbon in Sandra's hair or Victor's totally out-of-place outfit, Henrique drags me by the arm with a wide—maybe *too* wide—smile and yells, "I NEED TO GO TO THE BATHROOM, WHY DON'T YOU COME WITH ME?"

I try to stammer an answer, looking from him to Victor and Sandra, but before I can come up with anything, he pulls me with him, leaving a dumbfounded look on their faces and mine.

We cross the sea of people and manage to go up the stairs toward the bathrooms on the second floor, where there aren't as many people. Henrique pulls me inside by the hand and closes the door, and I find myself squeezed against him in a stall meant for one person. What is he doing? My God, he's not expecting we'll . . . stay in here together, right?

"Dude, I screwed up." He runs his hands over his sweaty face and stares at me, and I have no idea what he's talking about.

"Why did you lock us into a bathroom stall, Henrique? You realize the bouncers are going to throw us out of this party if they catch us, right?"

"Chill out, we're not doing anything and aren't going to, and— That's not the point!"

"Of course it is! If Victor comes looking for you and sees you locked in here with someone else, what do you think is gonna go through his mind?"

Henrique stares at me, and it feels like one of those cartoon scenes where the character discovers something obvious that he wasn't able to realize by himself.

"You're right, so I gotta be quick." He shoves his hand into his pocket and pulls out his phone. "I sent Victor a voice message. It's bad. Really bad."

"Did he listen to it yet?"

"Not yet. At least I don't think so. If he had, he wouldn't be here."

Bad Luck must be both our middle names. "But what did you say in it?"

Henrique summarizes the content in incoherent sentences, but I get the gist.

"Ah" is all I can say.

"Yeah. Ah. And that's why you need to help me. I need you to delete the message from his phone before he can listen to it."

"What? How do you expect me to do that?"

"I don't know, man, I don't know! I'm out of options here, Ian, and I really like him, but I'm so . . . frustrated and drunk and— Shit, he's going to listen to it and think I don't like him anymore, and then everything will be over."

Henrique unlocks the door, and we leave the stall under the judgmental eyes of a guy waiting in line. I have no idea what to do with myself, so I stare at the floor. When we start walking down the stairs to the main dance floor, I feel the floor give way again, then grab Henrique's shoulders.

If a fun evening to take my mind away from the bad stuff was what I wanted, I definitely got it.

Henrique stumbles on his own feet, and the only reason he doesn't tumble all the way down the stairs is because he's holding on to the handrail. I follow him, also holding on for dear life. I still haven't had a single beer inside the club, but it's as if I've just finished my eighth can. It's not quite the same as being drunk: Things pass by faster, but I can still hold on to my memories and am very well aware of what I'm doing. I just feel dizzy, really dizzy, and my body temperature is higher than usual, but my consciousness is still intact.

Henrique, on the other hand, is out of his mind, but he notices I'm searching for support and following his steps.

"Are you drunk?" he asks. "Great. So now one drunk guy will try to help another drunk guy not screw himself. That's really great!"

"I'm not drunk!" I retort, and his expression says that's exactly the answer he'd expect from a drunk guy. "I got started on the meds today! I'm just dizzy."

It's bizarre to say it openly and naturally. The music is so loud I had to scream it, but I'm not afraid someone will hear me.

Henrique freezes and looks me in the eye. He props me against a wall and leans on my shoulder.

Great. Now Victor is going to see us, and I'm certain he'll think we're kissing.

"Are you serious?" He stares at me, and he seems almost sober now. "Shit, it's true!"

"Is that a bad thing?"

"No, it's just . . ." He takes a deep breath and tries to organize his thoughts. "I invited you tonight so you could get some distraction, keep your mind out of trouble. And then the first thing I do is get you involved in my own problems. That's not a great look for a friend."

"Dude, chill." I smile, maybe because he used the word *friend* without a second thought. He really seems bothered by the situation, and the booze is amplifying his feelings, putting him near that state where people start crying for no reason. It's a little funny, I have to admit, to see his eyes filling with sentimental tears. "This is way better than staying home and waiting for nightmares to come. I actually have to thank you for getting me out of the house. Now come on, we have work to do."

We complete the odyssey of getting down the stairs to the first floor. Victor and Sandra are dancing and drinking, still under the stairs. She gives me the stink eye, and Victor seems, more than anything, confused.

"VICTOR!" I scream in his ear when the transition brings the volume down a little. "MY PHONE RAN OUT OF BATTERY. CAN I BORROW YOURS?"

"WHAT?" he asks, confused.

It's the only idea I can come up with on such short notice. Sticking my hand in his pocket and grabbing his phone would be both inappropriate and inefficient, since most people keep their screens locked and I have no way of knowing his code. Stealing his phone and disappearing in the crowd or shattering it on the floor wouldn't be very cool of me. But if I could unlock the screen and pretend I'm making a call, I'm sure I can delete the damn audio.

"PHONE. I NEED TO BORROW ONE. CAN I USE YOURS?"

The music is so loud, and Victor nods but doesn't move to put his hand in his pocket and get his phone, which leads me to the conclusion he couldn't understand a single word I said.

But Sandra did. She looks from me to Henrique, suspicious, and narrows her eyes before I can ask for his phone a third time.

"YOU CAN HAVE MINE!" She flashes a pleasant smile and hands me the phone, already on the dial screen. Victor resumes his dancing, totally carefree, and doesn't even realize what's going on around him.

Henrique's eyes widen when he sees that Sandra is trying to hand me her phone, and in an act of desperation, he does the only thing his drunken mind can come up with as a reasonably acceptable idea.

"I LOVE THIS SONG!" he screams, spreading his arms buoyantly, aiming at Sandra's hand and, right on target, hitting her phone.

The phone flies across the dance floor as she screams:

"HEY, WHAT THE HELL?!"

I see the little black brick spinning in the air and landing on the floor amid the people dancing.

"OH GOD, SANDRA, I'M SO SORRY!" Henrique yells, and it's obvious he's not feeling even a little bit of remorse.

Henrique runs toward the phone he just knocked down, asking the crowd to let him pass. Sandra goes after him, staring daggers at me as if I were the one responsible.

"WHERE DID THEY GO?!" Victor looks around, frowning. "WHAT'S GOING ON?"

Before Victor can realize what's happening, the music stops completely, and the lights go off. Everyone starts booing at the sudden interruption, but the stage lights soon go on, and people switch to cheering.

Sandra retrieves her phone, and it seems intact. Henrique is practically kneeling beside her, apologizing. When I look over again, Henrique has disappeared toward the bar, and in less than a minute he comes back with two beers in an attempt to make amends. He hands one of the bottles to Sandra with an awkward smile. She stares at him suspiciously but accepts the beer and takes a sip.

"What happened?" asks Victor, in a normal tone of voice now that there's no music in the club, as soon as the two of them come back to where we are.

"A little accident, but all is well!" Henrique answers, making Sandra toast with him in a sign of peace.

Henrique's eyes fall on me again, begging me to continue trying to delete the message from Victor's phone.

I hate him so much right now.

"Victor, I wonder if I could use your phone to make a call? Mine ran out of battery."

"Sure!" he says, and I realize this is the first time he understands my request. Sandra does not complain or ask why I'm being so persistent about this, and Victor, oblivious, grabs his phone from his pocket and unlocks it. "The battery is about to die, so you'll have to be fast."

I smile with the phone in my hands, and I'm already ahead of the game, trying to find the app on the main screen. It's a total breach of privacy, and I'm absolutely certain it's not the right thing to do, but Henrique begged me to, and—

Victor's phone screen goes black, the battery dead.

Why the hell doesn't anyone in this group charge their freaking phones?!

# CHAPTER 14

# VICTOR

IAN HANDS ME THE PHONE. He seems a bit frustrated.

"What is it?" I ask.

"Out of battery."

"Oh, crap. I should have plugged it in before I left my house."

I'm not too worried, though, since Sandra is with me, and whenever my phone dies, my mom calls her to make sure I'm still alive.

I put the phone back in my pocket and turn my attention to the stage.

I step closer to Henrique, smiling, and hold his hand. We look at the stage and stay that way, like two silly lovebirds, hand in hand.

Silly. That's a bit how I feel when I'm by his side, as if my head were too light and floating across space, away from my worries. The fear now plays only a small cameo in something much larger and way more intense.

Love. Is that what I'm feeling, after all? This sensation that being next to him is the best feeling in the world, is this what the experts call *being in love*? I don't know if there's a rational definition or if what's in the dictionary corresponds precisely to this mix of emotions boiling inside me. All I know is that it feels good, that holding hands with him is the only thing I need right now. Not the sex we've already had, the kisses we've already exchanged, or the way we've been doing things up to this point, like we're in a nonlinear movie, but just this: intertwined fingers, his warm hand against my cold one, the silence as the two of us pay attention to the stage, the slight squeeze he gives my hand, signaling that the show is about to start.

"There's something I need to tell you." I hear his voice in my ear, and I lower my head a little so he doesn't have to strain his neck so much. His voice is a little slow, and I know he's drunk. "I didn't think you were going to come tonight . . ."

"I thought about not coming," I admit. "But something told me I would regret it."

He opens his mouth in a goofy smile. A drunk smile.

"And I might have . . . thought some things . . . and said some things that aren't true."

"What are you talking about?"

"I left you a message on—"

"Let's not talk about this right now," I say, because I don't want to think about our arguments. His breath on my ear is passionate and intense and sends shivers down the back of my neck. "I don't want to . . . think about what's in the past."

So I come closer to his lips and kiss them. At first he responds shyly, but little by little he increases the intensity, as if he wants us to become one. And that kiss shows me how I'm not the only one who's vulnerable, not the only one who's afraid and doesn't know what his future is going to look like, not the only one trying to be happy, despite all things conspiring against that happiness.

We pull away when the music and lights become frantic and smoke from the stage takes over the entire club. Two strong men—naked except for golden speedos, just like the creature Frank-N-Furter created—come up, carrying a folded carpet, the ends of it propped on their shoulders. I know exactly what's about to happen, thanks to Sandra's pressuring me to watch *Cleopatra*, even though the movie is over three hours long.

The two men put the carpet down, and everyone seems dumb-founded.

Amateurs.

The rug starts moving, and people cheer. The men in golden speedos help unfold the carpet, and from within rises Cleopatra, the queen of the night, with her blue dress, straight black hair falling to her shoulders, her head adorned in gold, makeup outlining her eyes with electric-blue contacts.

"There are never enough hours in the days of a queen, and her nights have too many," she says softly before the music bursts into our ears.

The crowd claps and cheers when Bibi Montenegro starts walking from one side to the other, lip-syncing to a song and making everyone laugh. She's perfect onstage. Her dark skin shines with the gold in her makeup and ornaments; she's a moving jewel, and each step she takes seems to have been designed to highlight her best poses. People get their cameras out for pictures and videos, and she really does look like a queen.

The music ends, and people won't stop clapping. Her forehead is covered in sweat and her chest comes up and down with heaving breaths, but her smile communicates that exhaustion is a small price to pay for the joy of being up there in this moment.

She brings her mic to her lips. "I am the Nile!" she says in a powerful voice, making everyone scream even louder, which is hard to believe is possible. "I will have sons. Isis has told me."

When she says that, she lifts her head up and raises her hands, making her tunic flutter. The men in gold speedos unstrap the ties of the tunic, revealing a different outfit, this time a swimsuit covered in golden embroidery, like the grooves of a river on a map, and the other drag queens start walking in from both sides of the stage.

Everybody in the club goes wild.

The next song starts playing, and everyone starts dancing

rehearsed choreography, driving the audience to a complete frenzy. I see Henrique smile, proud of his friend in front of everyone, drawing her energy from the crowd's cheers. He holds me by the waist, and the two of us contemplate the noisy show in silence, and all I know that I don't want this night to ever end.

# CHAPTER 15

# HENRIQUE

MY MOUTH TASTES LIKE RUBBER.

My head is spinning.

My stomach feels like there's a rave going on inside it.

My God, I want to die.

I'll never ever drink another drop of alcohol.

I raise my hand toward the phone on the nightstand, unplug the charger, and check what time it is. It's eleven a.m., and the world hasn't stopped spinning yet. The last thing I remember is seeing Eric having the best night of his life, and the rest is in flashes: running into the bathroom and locking myself in the stall, throwing up all the wine, tequila, and beer; Sandra holding me as I say, "Nooo, I don't want to leeeave," even though the sun was already rising and the only people left in the club were the bouncers and the cleaning staff; and then devouring an overpriced hot dog while hearing Victor say I was in no condition to go home by myself and also where the hell was Eric? I vaguely recall Victor pushing me into a taxi and talking to a drag queen he didn't know, maybe Mad Madonna or Nicolle Lopez, who was kind enough to tell the driver where I live.

Victor. He was sitting next to me in the cab.

Oh, crap. He stayed over.

I raise my head too quickly and bring my hand to it, because the world is still spinning. My throat is dry, and I'm wearing the same pants and socks as last night. My shirt is hanging on the desk chair, and the sheets are on the floor, making an impromptu bed that no one is using.

I drag myself out of bed and hear someone talking outside. It's not Eric's or Victor's voice. It's Sandra's.

"You're not getting into an argument with him right now, Victor. You are not, and that's the end of it. He had no way of knowing you were going to show up."

"Did you hear what he said? My God, he said that before he saw me and then acted as if nothing had happened! And what was Ian trying to do? Use my phone to call someone in the middle of a club? He was trying to delete the message!"

Oh, crap.

"Good . . . morning," I say from the bedroom door, putting an immediate end to their discussion. Sandra looks at me with the expression of a lawyer who has tried all possible arguments for the defense but knows the cause is lost. "Did you sleep well?"

Neither of them says a word. My throat goes even drier.

"I don't know," Victor says. "I might have been sleeping too selfishly."

"Victor . . ." Sandra tries to steer away from the argument. "He's hungover. Don't do this now."

"No," I say as I walk into the kitchen. I pour myself some water and gulp it down quickly. "It's best if we do it now. Can we talk, Victor? Sandra, you can grab whatever you want from the fridge. And do your parents know you're here?" I ask Victor.

"I told them we stayed over at my brother's," Sandra answers on his behalf. "No need to worry about that."

"Great." I get more water and walk back to the bedroom door. "Shall we?"

Victor doesn't seem willing to talk, but Sandra gives him an encouraging wave, and he gets up from the couch. We go to the bedroom, and I close the door as soon as Victor walks by me.

"Is this the part where you apologize and tell me you didn't mean any of it and it was all the booze talking?" he asks, folding his arms in a defensive pose, then sitting on the bed with his legs crossed. "Because that's not gonna fly."

I place the glass of water on the desk, open the closet, and take out my morning medication. I pop the pill in my mouth and drink the second glassful.

"What is that?" he asks.

"It's my regular dose," I reply, trying to make the move seem as nondramatic as possible.

He laughs dryly. "Are you trying to calm me down?"

"I've done this every morning for the past three years, Victor. It's my daily routine."

I watch his green eyes stare at me, trying to process my routine and what it means. But the truth is, it doesn't mean anything other than what I just said: It's my daily routine.

"Well . . . ?" He lets the question hang in the air. "When does the 'I'm so sorry for what I said' speech start?"

I shrug. "I'm not sure I should apologize for what I said."

Another dry laugh. "You're pathetic."

"Is that what you really think?"

"Yes."

I remain silent, looking at him.

"Okay," I say.

"That's it?" He seems furious. "Your big apology is an *okay*?"

"I can't control how you feel or tell you that it's wrong, Victor. So, yeah, okay. I might be pathetic, but I don't regret anything I said in that message. That wasn't the booze talking. That was me, saying exactly what I think about everything that's going on between us. And if you're not capable of seeing that I am entitled to my feelings as well, things will never work out between us."

"Things will only work out between us if you start trusting other people, and it looks like you still don't."

"And can you blame me for that? I've trusted others before, believed that maybe it would all work out, but things have never ended well. And after so long trying to be optimistic, you can't help but get tired of it."

"So you don't believe me? You still don't believe that I really like you?"

"Of course I do! But not until last night, not until after all that silence. But, unlike everyone else, you came back."

"So you said all those things?"

"I said all those things," I confirm. "Can you ever understand?"

"I'm not sure I can. The things you said, they were . . ."

He seems uncertain about the proper adjectives, so I offer: "Cruel? Cold? Inconsiderate?"

His jaw tightens. "Exactly."

"Maybe now you'll understand how I feel every single day when someone disappears because they're too scared to be with me."

"You said I was scared. And selfish." More than angry, Victor seems hurt by my words. "How can you say all those things and then stand by my side as if you hadn't?"

"I stood by you because I enjoyed it. Because you surprised me by being different from all the other guys who have come and gone. What you can't understand, Victor, is that all this is new for me, too. Being with someone who knows who I am and still shows up, even with all the fear of what might happen in the future. This is different from what I've experienced in the last few years, when everyone just turned their backs and walked away."

"And what *you* can't seem to understand is that people have the right to be afraid. They have the right to not want to show up if they think that's what's best for them."

"There you go. That's exactly what I'm talking about. You're being selfish again."

"And you think you're so much better than everyone else, yeah? So superior with your 'I don't care, I don't apologize, I said exactly what I wanted to say.' So why the fuck did you try to get Ian to delete the message you sent? Or did you think I wouldn't realize what was going on?"

"Because I wanted to avoid . . . this!" I say, waving my hands about. "This pointless argument about who's more fragile and who's more selfish. But you know what? Now I'm happy that you listened to it."

"Happy? You're sick."

"I'm happy because now you know what I think every time someone new comes into my life and disappears like a fucking cloud of smoke. It's been three years of living with this fatigue, Victor. Three years of trying to convince myself that it's better to be alone than to face this kind of reaction and the silence that follows every time I mention those three magic letters. It's easy for you to turn around and walk away, but I still have to live with it every day."

"But you can't ignore the fact that people are scared!"

"I know! You think I wasn't terrified when I got my results? You think I didn't spend a whole week thinking this was a punishment from God, and that I deserved it? Scared is my middle name, Victor, but one thing I learned over these years is that fear is not a fifty-foot-tall monster I have to bow to. I'm afraid every single day: afraid my undetectable status will change; afraid that some political shit will happen and the meds will stop being distributed; afraid I'll have a cut inside my mouth and kiss someone who also has a cut inside their mouth; afraid that I'll tell someone I have HIV and that person will simply disappear, like I thought you were going to—*like you did*."

"But you can't act like you don't have any responsibility for what happened!" he screams, and I notice he's balled his hands into fists. "None of this would have happened if you'd been more careful. You can't be mad at me when this was all your fault!"

And there it is: the punch to the gut—the thing no one says but everyone thinks.

"I'm sorry, I . . ." He tries to lower his voice, then takes a step forward in an appeasing gesture.

But now I'm the one losing it. "Choice?" I raise my voice, telling my headache and hangover to just eat it. I can't believe what he just said. "You think this is a choice?!"

"It's the consequence of your actions, and you need to deal with it," he says in a low voice. So selfish. "I don't have to be dragged into all this shit just because I like you."

"Moron. You are nothing more than a spoiled brat who thinks he knows how the world works." I'm choking on the tears trying to stream down my face, but I hold them back. "Get out of my house."

He stares at me and doesn't budge.

"Out," I repeat. I don't want to talk anymore; I don't want to hear one more word or look at his face, not now, not ever.

"So that's how you're going to deal with—"

"OUT!" I lose it, charging to the bedroom door and yanking it open. "NOW!"

Sandra sees the scene from the couch, her eyes wide when she raises her head, totally forgetting about whatever she was checking on her phone.

Victor raises his hands and takes long strides toward the living room without making another sound. He grabs his things from the table, shoves them all in his pocket as quickly as he can, and calls to Sandra, who remains silent. She doesn't ask what happened but looks at me doubtfully, and I glare back, annoyed.

Eric arrives as they are heading out. He's carrying a backpack and still has some leftover makeup on his face, the look of someone who probably met a fan who made sure his night was much better than mine. Sandra and Victor don't say anything as they take the stairs down.

"Hey, what's the rush?" he asks with a smile. Then he walks into the apartment and sees me, still standing in my bedroom, breathing heavily. "Was there a fire?"

I don't wait for him to come closer. Instead, I walk to him and bury my face in his shoulder, letting all the tears out.

"Oh, Henrique" is all he manages to say, squeezing me into his slender body as my chest heaves uncontrollably. I can't breathe, but I can't stop crying, either.

And I don't ever want to stop.

# CHAPTER 16

# IAN

THERE'S NO ONE BY MY side when I take my medicine the second time.

The process is the same: At first, lying in bed, everything seems fine, but as soon as I get up to go to the bathroom, the world starts spinning like I'm an ice skater performing a triple axel. I lean against walls and furniture as best I can, trying to hide what's happening. It's as if I were drunk.

The doctor said it gets better with time. And for heaven's sake, I need it to get better.

Then come the nightmares. When I least expect them, they're there, tormenting me with their bizarre, nonsensical imagery.

The first is of a woman dressed in red. She's standing, and even in the darkness, I can see her dress floating at her feet, her dark hair falling over her shoulders. She steps closer, little by little, and I notice her face has no eyes, nose, or mouth. Yet I can feel it when her skin comes close to mine, radiating heat and making me sweat so much that it stains the pillow.

I wake up in terror, my heart fluttering, body drenched in sweat, throat dry. I don't want to get up for more water because I know I'm going to bump into every single piece of furniture in the apartment and wake everyone up. So I pull the sheets off me and open the window, softly so I don't wake Vanessa.

I pray for a breeze that doesn't come and, lying on my back, look up at the ceiling. I feel my eyelids get heavy as time passes, and I stare at the shadows appearing on the ceiling from the few streetlights outside. The tree branches form hands that become arms, and I can see fingers flexing and coming to life, changing from a pattern in the concrete to a three-dimensional form in the darkness. It's as if the shadows have come to life and started moving forward, and then they grab me by the neck and suffocate me.

I cough and open my eyes again. My second nightmare.

*It will get better with time*, I think again. *Everything is going to be all right.*

I really want that to be true.

+

The next few days don't go much better. Not just because of the sleepless nights—sleepless more out of fear that the nightmares will come back than of the nightmares themselves, since they have been happening less—but also because of my mood swings.

The first one I'm able to recognize happens on a Wednesday evening, and I have no idea what makes me act like such a jerk. Vanessa is sitting on the bedroom floor, as usual, with books scattered all around her, spirals of DNA drawn on ruled paper, and the radio on with her classical music cranked all the way up.

I walk to the radio and turn it off.

"I can't hear myself think!" I say, annoyed, lying down in my bed and closing my eyes, feeling the weight of the world crashing down upon me. Gravity annoys me.

"Hey! I'm trying to study!" she complains when the sounds from the street, as well as of my mom and dad talking about whatever is on the evening news, waft into the room.

With my mom in the living room and my dad in the bedroom and the TV loud enough for both of them to hear it, their conversation isn't exactly quiet.

"Put in your earbuds," I grumble, and she swears but unwillingly takes her phone out, plugs in the earbuds, and starts the music again.

Cranked up to the highest volume.

I try to ignore the loud noise coming from her earbuds, but I can't. One of my feet seems agitated, going up and down as the violins roar and echo in a bothersome clatter that seems to enter my head like nails on a chalkboard.

"Vanessa, turn the volume down!" I yell, but she doesn't hear me. She's too focused, her head bobbing, scribbling down her dominant and recessive genes. "Vanessa! VANESSA!"

I get up and rip the earbuds out of her ears.

"I can't hear myself think!" I say again.

"And why is that *my* problem?! Leave me alone!" she complains, retrieving her tangled earbuds from the floor and looking at the copper from the bare wire on one of the ends. "Look at what you've done!" She shows me the mangled earbud I broke when I pulled it.

"I told you to lower the volume on that crap twice, and you couldn't even hear me!"

"How old are you, Ian? I need to study here; how hard can that be to understand?"

"I can't understand how you can study with all this noise in your head! Do you think you're going to get into college if you can't even concentrate when someone is talking right next to you?"

"That's none of your business!"

We're raising our voices more than usual, louder than the TV in the living room, which our mom notices.

"What's going on in here?" she asks, opening the door to our room and looking from Vanessa's crossed arms and her mad expression to me, impatient.

"Who knows?" is Vanessa's honest answer. "Ian must have stepped on a nail and decided to take it out on me!"

"Ian?" My mother shoots me a questioning look.

"My God, can't the two of you leave me alone for one single moment?" I put on my flip-flops, grab my phone, which was lying next to my pillow, and leave.

I walk to the front door and turn the key to unlock it.

"Where are you headed, buddy?" my dad asks, more curious than disapproving.

"Anywhere that's not here!" I say, leaving and slamming the door behind me.

My house is suffocating. I know I'm acting childish, but the mix of sounds and heat bothers me, making my head spin in a type of nausea that is not a side effect of the medicine—or maybe it is and I just don't want to admit it. I'm unsure about whether I want to take the elevator or the stairs, then choose the second option and manage to go down only two flights before I have to stop, hold on to the rail, and take a deep breath with my eyes closed. My heart is beating fast, and sweat is running down my temples. It feels like the universe is crushing my body.

I squeeze the phone in my hand and sit down in the silent staircase, praying no gossipy neighbors will decide to use it right this moment and ask me what the matter is. There are two cigarette butts on the floor from someone who couldn't be bothered to throw them out. I kick them while going through my contacts list, searching for Gabriel's name.

I scroll down through *G* and get to *H*, where I see Henrique's name. Before I can think it through, he's the one I'm calling.

"Hello?" the voice on the other end says after the second ring.

"Is it always this bad?" I ask, skipping the whole "Hey, how're you doing? I'm fine, and you?" preamble.

"Hello to you, too, Ian," he answers sarcastically.

"I don't know if I can do this, Henrique."

He knows what I mean. It's not just the medicine or the side effects or the mood swings or the shortness of breath. It's the fear and loneliness, the secrets and this annoying tendency to worry about what other people think.

"If you keep thinking about giving up before you even try, you're probably right." He says this with a soft voice, as if he were one of those bosses who fires an incompetent employee on staff, all while wearing a friendly smile on his face. And yet, I feel the words like a slap in the face; they're so different from what I expected to hear.

I remain silent.

"But if you think there's more to life than that, then everything will work out," he continues, his voice softer.

"I'm so . . . pissed at the world!" I say, unsatisfied, wanting him to tell me the formula to put an end to this feeling. How can he seem so calm when it feels like everything is falling apart?

"Welcome to the club," he says with a hint of sarcasm.

"Does it get better?"

"If you let it, it does. Give yourself time to get used to these changes, Ian, and try not to lash out at people, as hard as that might sound. No one else has anything to do with your problems."

"Including you," I say, noting the impatience in his voice.

He laughs. "I already told you: You can count on me, you idiot. After helping me this weekend, you scored some extra points. Not that it did much, but at least you tried."

"So that's what it is."

"What?"

"That's why you're in such a bad mood."

"I'm not in a bad mood."

"Henrique, I'm in a bad mood, and misery loves company."

This time, Henrique lets out a weary sigh. "Maybe," he answers.

"You want to talk?"

"Have you noticed that every time we start talking about your problems, we end up talking about mine? It's now our routine."

"What can I say? Your life is much more interesting."

"I wish."

Then silence.

"So . . ." I let it hang for a moment. "Why the bad mood? What happened between you and Victor?"

"It wasn't quite a scene from a Tessa Dare romance novel," he grumbles. "It was more of a Nicholas Sparks kind of fight. The type that doesn't make a lot of sense."

"That bad?"

"That bad."

So he gives me the broad strokes, in a low, sad voice, of what Victor said to him. I feel my entire body prickle.

"I don't know if I want to see him again," Henrique concludes in a clearly dispirited voice.

"You're giving up before you even try?" I ask.

"Hey, that's my line!" He lets out what is supposed to be a laugh. "But this is different."

"No, it's not."

"He hurt me."

"People hurt each other every day, Henrique. I just hurt my sister over something really idiotic."

"What he said to me . . . I don't know if that's something I should forgive. That I *can* forgive."

"So you like to hold on to your grudges?"

"No, that's not what it is, it's just that . . . it's so exhausting. I wish everything could be . . . *normal*, you know?"

"We have to start getting used to the fact that our normal is not the same as the normal we see in Hollywood movies."

"That would be so much better."

"I think you can look at it in two ways: You can forget that Victor exists and stop talking to him, and eventually find someone who will make you happy, because after all, there are seven billion people on this planet, and not all of them can be jerks; or you can talk to him, because I know you like each other, and try to figure it out the best way you can. I'm going to get very cliché now and say I think this is the time to listen to your heart to see if it's worth staying with Victor. Has he tried calling you yet?"

"At least fifteen times. He left a bunch of texts, too, but I haven't read any of them."

"Well, at least he's trying."

"But what if he's just another disappointment, Ian? Let's assume I start talking to him again. How long until he rubs it in my face and hurts me again? How long before he uses my past as an obstacle to our future?"

"I don't know. You don't know, either, and I bet Victor doesn't. But there's a difference between being in a relationship where we know the other person is no good for us and being in one with someone who made a mistake. From everything you told me about

Victor, he's immature, but he makes you feel good. He said some shitty things, and I don't want you to let him think that there's any excuse for that, but at the end of the day, it was a mistake. And mistakes must be forgiven, as hard as it is to get over them."

"Whoa."

"What?"

"I didn't know you were taking psychology classes. Aren't you a math major?"

"Economics. People think it's math, but it's actually a social science. And we have an economic-thinking class. It's the closest we get to trying to understand how the human mind works."

"It's working out. You could start your own practice."

"If nothing else works out, I'll sell my advice on the beach."

I realize we're reaching that point where silence will take over the conversation, but I don't want to hang up. I hear Henrique's breathing on the other side of the line, and it soothes me. When I hear about his problems, I realize that we're both deep in our own crises and paranoias and that talking about them is helpful; it makes everything more bearable.

"Ian?" Henrique asks after almost ten seconds, during which I am lost in these reflections.

"What?"

"Just making sure you were there."

"I'm still here but have to get going. I walked out of our apartment in a panic, and I'm sure my mom is wondering what happened."

"Okay. Take care, all right?"

"Thanks, Henrique. For everything."

And I hang up the phone, feeling weary.

I go back to my apartment after taking about a dozen deep breaths.

"Is everything okay, Ian?" my mom asks as soon as I walk in, dragging my feet and looking at her with an embarrassed grin on my face.

"I just needed to get some air. Finals start next week."

"You'll end up having a heart attack if you're still stressed like that when you turn nineteen."

"The apple doesn't fall far from the tree," I say with a grin, and drag myself back into the bedroom.

Vanessa has turned off the lights and is already in bed, looking at her phone. She scrolls through Instagram, taps a picture twice, scrolls a bit more, smiles, narrows her eyes, taps twice, and keeps scrolling.

I walk up to her bed and lie down next to her without saying a word. She doesn't complain or ask what I think I'm doing but moves over to give me more space, still staring at her screen. Scrolls down, taps twice, smirks.

"I'm sorry," I mumble, gazing at the beams under my bunk bed. "I was kind of a jerk, wasn't I?"

"A huge jerk," she says.

I want to have a conversation with her. Tell her about my life, my problems, keep her up to date so she won't think I'm just an annoying older brother.

"I know" is all I can say.

She turns off her phone and remains still, now looking up, too.

"Do you think I'm going to get in, Ian?"

"What?"

"Into college. Sometimes it feels like I'm studying so hard, but nothing is sticking. Sometimes it seems like it's all a series of things that don't make sense that other people are able to understand, but I'll never be as good as they are."

So here she is, making my selfishness blatantly obvious. This whole time I've been thinking only my problems mattered. She's also a ball of anxiety with expectations for the future, kind of like I was when I was taking my college admission exams.

"Of course you'll get in, Vanessa. If that's what you want and you try really hard, there's nothing you can't accomplish."

I'm not sure I'm speaking the truth, but it seems like the right thing to say right now.

I pull her into a hug, and she buries her head in my shoulder.

"You're still a jerk," she mumbles, closing her eyes.

"I know," I answer, also closing mine. "But I'm *your* jerk."

I fall asleep right there, and that night, there are no nightmares.

# CHAPTER 17

# VICTOR

I CAN'T GET THE IMAGE of Henrique's expression when he told me to leave his apartment off my mind. I twist and turn in bed, thinking about how everything I said was unfair, and I rehearse conversations in my head where I try to apologize sincerely. I realize, way too late, that my words were cruel, but the worst part is that his eyes had an exhaustion about them the moment he heard those words, as if he'd known that, sooner or later, I'd become just another disappointment in his life. It must have seemed to him that my words came from a script—a story he was all too used to hearing.

I pick up my phone and stare at all the apologetic messages I sent. All read (or at least seen), but none replied to. I scan the list of recent calls and see that his name fills the entire screen, with different time tags. Mechanically, I press the phone icon and try calling one more time, bringing the phone up to my ear. It rings once, twice, ten times, then goes to voice mail. I don't leave a message.

This might be a sign that I shouldn't try to contact him anymore. I think he's made it clear that he doesn't want to talk to me, and I don't know if I can blame him. Our relationship was set up to fail from the start.

So that's that. Onward. Take a deep breath, Victor. Other guys will come into your life; more opportunities will come. All you need to do is give it time, and hope things will get better.

I put my phone on the nightstand and notice the *Pet Sematary* Blu-ray case he gave me on our second date, the one with the *Transformers* disc inside. I grab the blue box, open it, and see the note he scribbled.

*The greatest horror movie of all time.*

I smile at the memories of when things were easier. Of when I'd stare at my phone, hoping to hear from him, wondering how someone could come into my life and, in such little time, become so important. Of when the text would finally come—a simple "What you up to tonight?"—and I was certain he had been thinking about me, too, perhaps waiting for the right moment to reach out. And when we'd go out and walk hand in hand, unafraid of anyone or anything, everything seemed right in the world. It was the first time I had felt such a strong connection with someone, and there was no use in trying to find an explanation for what I'd been feeling, because there was none. All I knew was that I was with someone who made me happy simply by existing, and I wanted to feel like that as often as possible. The silly clichés suddenly made sense when we were together, and every single one applied to the two of us.

But that's over now.

I take a deep breath and try to relax, repeating to myself that I shouldn't think about Henrique or what I said to him. I shouldn't think about the things that happened between us or the expression in his dark eyes or those lips that used to smile so widely but that in my last memory alternated between anger and disappointment.

I can't think about him. I have to think of myself. It's for the best, isn't it? Our relationship was never going to work out.

I should think of myself.

I should think of myself.

So why can't I stop thinking about him?

+

"Any idea what you're going to do, Victor?"

We're in our video production class, and Sandra pokes me with her pen, scratching her head with the other hand as she stares at the piece of paper on the table in front of her.

The professor left to get coffee, and everyone is chatting, but I didn't pay attention to the directions, so I have no idea what all the commotion is about.

"What?" I ask, staring at the piece of paper. I still haven't read the instructions.

"Are you paying attention?"

"No."

She rolls her eyes and sighs. "The professor is assigning us a new project."

"Oh, yeah?" I scan the instructions quickly. We have to come up with a script for a short film, no longer than five minutes, on a theme of our choosing. "Cool."

Sandra gives me a dubious look, as though wondering if I did any drugs before coming to this class.

"Is everything okay, Victor?"

"Yeah," I answer unconvincingly.

"It's Henrique, isn't it? Have you talked to him yet?"

"I don't want to talk about him, Sandra."

"So it didn't work out, or you just haven't discussed it with him yet?"

"We haven't spoken. And I don't want to talk about it," I repeat.

"But I do. Let's go outside and grab coffee."

Without waiting for my answer, she gets up and leaves the room. I follow her.

We sit down in front of Miss Irene's yellow trailer, and Sandra makes a hand gesture, asking her for two coffees. Our professor is there talking to another professor and smoking a cigarette. If she notices us, she doesn't bother asking us to get back to class when she says goodbye to the man and heads back to the classroom.

Sandra lights a cigarette when the coffees arrive. She pours half the sugar container into her cup, then hands me the jar, and I pour just a little bit to cut the bitterness.

"I think I don't want anything to do with him anymore," I say, breaking the silence when I notice Sandra only stares at me, waiting until I say something. "Shouldn't relationships be about one's happiness and feeling good? I think all these hiccups are the universe telling us we need some distance between us."

"You don't really believe that, do you?"

"That Henrique and I need some space?" I shrug. "Maybe."

"No. In the signs-from-the-universe crap. About you thinking there's something bigger out there defining all the things that might happen in your life and basing your decisions on that. It's not very smart."

"I know."

"You regret having said those things to him, don't you?"

It's not quite a question. The look on my face is more than enough to show that if I could go back in time, I would. And Sandra knows that.

"I was a jerk."

"You were. But I've also been thinking over the last couple of days that this can't be easy for you, either."

I raise my eyebrows in surprise. Sandra is always the first to say things would get easier if I let them, and that all the complications between Henrique and me can be traced back to my fear, my prejudice, my lack of information.

"We're kind of a construction of everyone else's fears, you know," she continues, swirling the coffee cup, cigarette held firmly between her index and middle fingers. "We hear so much about HIV, and there are so many negative preconceptions associated with it that it's a little hard to think about how things today are vastly different from how they were thirty years ago. Even though

I only have a supporting role in this story, I sometimes catch myself thinking about it, too, and I try to put myself in your or Henrique's shoes. But the truth is, I can only *try* to do that, because when it comes down to it and I see myself in a situation like yours, there's no advice in the world that can make the things we're taught to think disappear overnight. Your fears are just yours, just as his are his alone."

"I didn't want things to end this way between us. I feel bad that I said what I did. All I want is for everything to turn out okay, even if Henrique and I never get to kiss each other again. I feel like a piece of shit."

"Have you tried talking to him?"

"I've sent a million texts and called a dozen times, but he's not responding."

"Okay, but I mean . . . have you tried *talking* to him?" she asks again, changing the emphasis.

"Like, face-to-face?"

"Yeah."

"People still do that, don't they?" I ask with a smile, trying to be funny. But Sandra doesn't laugh, so I shrug. "He didn't get back to me. I doubt he wants to see me."

"You can try."

We finish our coffee and go back into the classroom.

Sandra is right. I can try.

+

This might be the worst idea in the history of bad ideas.

It's Sunday afternoon, and I'm staring at the entrance to Henrique's building. I'm under one of the few remaining trees on the street, which is otherwise suffocated by concrete and cars parked on the curb. I look like a stalker from a TV show, checking out his ex-boyfriend's home and analyzing his routines, planning to do something awful to him.

I brush away these thoughts and cross the street without looking, only to almost get hit by a cyclist who swerves out of the way, cursing me. My heart was already out of control before, and now it sounds like the drumline of a samba school. I wipe the sweat off my forehead and take a deep breath, counting to three before I press 204 on the intercom.

I wait, but no one answers it. I press again, this time for longer, wondering if Henrique looked out the window and saw me down here or if there's simply no one at home.

Still no answer.

Frustrated, I start walking back to where I came from, when suddenly I hear Eric's voice on the intercom.

"Who is it?"

His voice sounds impatient and grumpy, as if he's just gotten out of bed and dragged himself to answer it.

"Eric?" I ask.

"The one and sleepy only. Who is this?" he asks again.

"It's Victor. I was wondering if I could . . . come upstairs and talk to Henrique?"

"Right now?"

"Right now."

The intercom goes silent for a few seconds.

"Did you call him and set up a time?" Eric asks in a serious voice, and I wonder if he's joking.

"N-no . . . He hasn't been answering any of my calls."

"And you don't think that means something?"

"Maybe it means that we need to talk in person so I can apologize," I answer.

This makes Eric go silent for a few more seconds.

"Hello? Eric?" I don't get a response and am about to press the intercom again, but I hear the click of the door unlocking.

I grin and climb the two flights of stairs to the apartment. As soon as I turn into the hallway, I see Eric standing in the open doorway, his slender, elegant arms crossed over a pink Hello Kitty shirt, his eyes those of someone who most likely just woke up.

"I'll leave the two of you alone," he says, and I wonder if he doesn't mind going out into the street in those pajamas (before I reach the conclusion that of course he doesn't). "If you do anything to hurt my friend even more, I will turn your life into a living hell."

It's not an empty threat but a real warning. My shoulders tense because I never thought Eric could be so serious, but I nod.

"Byesies!" he says with a smile, then puts on the sunglasses that were hanging from his collar before shooting down the stairs.

I step into the apartment and dodge the piles of clothes everywhere, looking for Henrique. He's not in the living room, but the apartment isn't that big, and I can see him on his bed with a book in front of him.

I take three more steps toward the doorframe, and Henrique looks up.

"May I come in?" I ask.

He closes the book and puts it on the nightstand, then hoists himself up to the middle of the bed, crossing his legs.

I take another step into the bedroom.

"Why didn't you reply to any of my texts?" I ask, putting my hands in my pockets. The desk chair is free, but I don't feel comfortable enough to sit, so I stay standing up, looking at Henrique's brown eyes and short hair, not knowing exactly what to say next.

"Because I don't want to deal with it. Not again. I thought I made that clear enough."

"You did."

"And yet, here you are, after saying the things you said."

"I feel like an idiot, Henrique. I need you to listen to me, because I . . . I feel like garbage. I have to apologize. What I said was not fair."

Henrique gives me a weary smile. "We say a lot of stuff when we're not thinking, but maybe that's exactly what we really want to say. I'm not harboring any resentments, Victor."

That's what his mouth says, but his inflection seems to contradict his words. His tone of voice is calm, sober, and almost flat, and all I want is to shake him. I want him to yell at me, to call me an idiot, to tell me I was a jerk. I want him to go through full catharsis and, in the end, say he forgives me. That he wants to forget the whole story and move on. I want him to kiss me and tell me everything's all right, or that, even if it isn't, things will get better.

But that's not what he says, not what he does. Instead, he remains in the same defensive pose, as if he were a freaking

Buddhist monk, calm and collected, rational and cold. And that's worse than any yelling or finger-pointing.

"No, Henrique. I didn't mean any of that. I was just . . . angry. At everything. Frustrated because of what happened, so I ended up lashing out at you. The things you said to me in that voice message . . . they really hurt, too." He remains silent, maybe thinking about his own mistakes. "But I don't mean to say that one mistake minimizes the other. What I said was unforgivable and cruel, and for a few days I tried to convince myself that it would be best to try and forget you and move on with my life, but I can't. I can't stop thinking about you and how good you make me feel."

"I thought a lot about you over the last week, too, Victor. About how every relationship is a new learning opportunity, no matter how old we are, and how everything is a big, new surprise. Maybe we are disappointed because we expect other people to say what we want to hear, but everyone has a right to say what they think, cruel as it might be."

I take another step toward Henrique, sit down on his bed, and look him in the eyes.

He smiles.

"I don't want you to think I'm that kind of person, Henrique," I say. "I'm sorry, and I want to learn from you. I don't want a stupid virus to stand in the way of our relationship, because we can't give it that kind of power."

"I don't," Henrique replies. "But people seem to insist on giving power to insignificant things."

"Can you forgive me?"

"I have nothing to forgive, Victor. Forgive what, your thoughts? I can't do that. But I don't want you to think I'm angry, because I'm not. That's the best I can do."

His words sound sober and sensible, but he still seems defensive, as if he's studied from a script with politically correct sentences to be said out loud. He seems numb, almost on autopilot.

And that scares me.

"Are we okay?" I ask.

"We are," he answers, but the words aren't soothing to me. "You'll find someone special, Victor. Someone with whom it's not this complicated."

That's when I realize this is not a reconciliation.

"I already have someone special in my life. That's you," I manage to say.

"It's not me, Victor. I'm complicated. Our relationship is complicated."

"I don't care. I'm not here because I want a weight off my shoulders, Henrique. I want you. I want to make new mistakes and learn from them; I want to be by your side and to show you that I'm not perfect, but I can still be special, because you are special to me. I love you."

That lights up something inside him, but not the way I wanted. There's no switch I can flip to change the course of this conversation, but I notice my words seem to move him somehow.

He reaches for my hands. "You're a special guy, Victor. But I can't give you the happiness you want so badly."

I want him to say he loves me, too. I want him to pull me into a hug and kiss me and tell me that nothing will keep us apart. I can't accept that these words are what he really wants.

"Of course you can! We can be happy, Henrique. We have to try, no matter the cost! What do you want from me? I want to prove to you that I am capable of changing—of growing—but I need you to trust me. Please, Henrique, I don't want to . . . not be with you."

He lets out a weary sigh and releases my hands. "We weren't meant to be, Victor."

"Stop saying that like you know what's best for me! I want to be with you; is that not enough?"

"No, it's not. Because I don't know if I want to be with you."

"Of course you do!"

"Now you're the one talking as if you knew what's best for me."

His coldness annoys me. I swallow hard.

"So this is it, then?" I ask, getting off the bed. "This is how things end between us?"

"Things never started, to be honest. We're better off apart."

"Speak for yourself," I say, trying to hold back tears. All of a sudden, the bedroom seems too small, and the walls seem to compress and suffocate me, little by little. This isn't how I imagined things going. It isn't how I believed this conversation would end. "I know I'm much better with you around."

"Goodbye, Victor." He reaches for the book and picks up where he left off.

He seems serene, as if the whole conversation was meaningless, as if the two of us were nothing but a casual affair that came to an end, the type of weak summer rain that leaves no trace behind.

Now I'm the one who wants to scream at him. Who wants to say that he's the one making any kind of closeness between us impossible, that he's the big jerk in this story, with or without HIV.

I'm capable of making him happy. I know I am. But right now, in this moment, when I turn my back to his apartment door and go down the stairs, not wanting to look at anything or anyone, I also don't know if I am capable of being happy without him.

## CHAPTER 18

# HENRIQUE

WHEN VICTOR LEAVES, I HEAVE a deep sigh of relief. It's impossible to focus on the book I'm reading or to think about anything other than him.

*I can't stop thinking about you and how good you make me feel.*

I know I was a jerk, but it was for the best. He needed to get away from me. That was the conclusion I reached while we weren't speaking. No matter how much he says he wants to be with me. I don't want him to be a part of the constant maelstrom of feelings I've become. I'm tired of trying to make everything work out, and I know that sooner or later during a fight or when things aren't going well, the cruelty will rear its ugly head and rub those words in my face.

*You wanted these things to happen.*

*This was your choice.*

*If only you'd been more careful.*

*If you hadn't had sex with every guy you saw in front of you.*

*Pervert.*

*Dirty.*

*I already have someone special in my life. That's you.*

I need to get my life back on track. It feels like I'm being diag-nosed all over again, and I don't know what to do with myself. Victor has made me as confused as I was in the first couple of days after I learned my status, my head spinning with what the future held for me.

*We have to try and be happy, no matter the cost!*

I still want to, but I'm starting to wonder if my happiness needs to be tied to a relationship. I have friends, a job, and a cha-otic apartment, don't I? I have my TV shows and movies, my songs and books, my medicine and my appointments with the doctor. That's all I need to fill my moments of boredom, to widen my horizons, to stay healthy and make sure the bad times go by unnoticed.

*Henrique, I don't want to . . . not be with you.*

I want to convince myself that I have a safety net ready to save me in case I decide to jump, but I'm not sure that's enough. I don't want to be one of those people who only feels complete when there's someone by their side, and yet it's inevitable to think about all the good things that could come from someone being there. But no, I can't think about it.

*I love you.*

I love you, too, Victor. But I wish everything were different.

+

I decide to focus on work, to become one of those people with a rigid routine, a time to wake up and one to go to bed, no moment to go off script for a dinner or a casual conversation at the bus stop. I go to work, come home, go into my bedroom, eat my meals, and watch TV, surviving without living, forgetting to look both ways and about the good things that exist around me.

I have an appointment with the doctor on Wednesday, and I go straight from work to his office to get my latest test results and talk. Dr. Glauco has been treating me since I was diagnosed, and with time he's become a good friend. He's one of those people who's interested in what you have to say, asking questions not because he's supposed to but because he really wants to know. He's bald, and his head is shaped like an egg; he has a salt-and-pepper beard and wears glasses with thick lenses that magnify his pitch-black irises. His dark skin is smooth and shows no signs that he's almost seventy, and his toned body makes him appear younger than fifty.

"Henrique!" He welcomes me with a hug instead of a hand-shake and pats the top of my head like a grandfather would his grandchildren. "How have you been?"

"Great!" I smile to hide my feelings, which I am now a pro at.

"Shall we take a look at your exams?" he asks, pulling out his chair and sitting as he opens my file. He spends a few seconds with the results and nods. "All great, as always." He circles my viral load of fewer than fifty copies and my CD4 levels, which are over six hundred. "It's looking like you'll outlive me by a while, boy!"

"I know you're a healthy man, but that is more or less what I have been aiming for," I answer.

He laughs and asks for my blood work next. I've already opened the file and taken a peek, so I know everything is fine with me.

"Have you been exercising?" he asks, because he knows of my sedentary lifestyle and the long hours at work, where sometimes I stay late into the night.

"You always have to pick on me for something! But I've started taking the stairs up to work instead of the elevator. Is that good enough?"

"That's a start, but you should be ashamed of yourself, Henrique! You live right next to a gym that's open until midnight. I don't believe you can't find some way of going there at least three times a week!"

I don't know why I decided to be friends with this guy and tell him every detail about my personal life. He always ends up using it as ammunition.

"My test results are great, stop judging me!"

"I'm not judging you!" he answers, still smiling, then closes the file. He writes a prescription for the next couple of months of medicine and hands it to me. "Everything is well, it seems. How about the boys?"

"Seriously?" I ask. "What are you, my great-aunt?"

"I'm already sixty-seven, all my sons are married, and my

grandkids aren't old enough for me to nag them with this kind of question yet." He shrugs. "All I have are my patients."

"There's no one in sight," I answer.

"So things didn't work out with that boy you mentioned during our last appointment?"

Damn. Why is his memory so good? I forgot I'd mentioned Victor to him.

"Too immature to deal with all that's going on in my life." I decide not to share any details. "But it's okay."

"Is it?" He seems skeptical.

"Mhm," I answer, not inviting the conversation.

"If nothing happened with him, I'm sure it will with a more mature and understanding someone."

"Yeah," I say, resigned. I don't know if that is the truth.

+

I'm about to enter the apartment, my stomach is growling, and I'm thinking about the yakisoba leftovers in the fridge but also about starting to go to the gym next Monday. I remember how Victor wrinkled his nose at yakisoba, and he said it tasted like something straight out of a squid's intestine. I can't help but laugh as I remember his face when I ordered a giant serving at a Japanese restaurant we went to after the movies, before everything started falling apart.

It's impossible not to think of him. At least that's what I think as I turn the key and walk into the living room.

I lose my appetite when I see Eric's uncomfortable look. He's sitting in the living room armchair with his hands on his knees, looking at a short blond guy unsuccessfully trying to make conversation. He's younger than me and has tanned skin and perfect teeth that form a blinding smile. His full blond beard is longer than it was the last time I saw him and is messy in a way that looks somehow lazy and purposeful at the same time. He's wearing a white T-shirt that reveals his arms and he has a Maori tattoo (also new) that reaches from his left shoulder all the way to his fist, covering the skin in between. His leg bounces up and down as he tries to talk to Eric, but I can see he's impatient.

"Henrique, hmm . . . we have a visitor," Eric says as soon as I walk in, looking at Carlos, my ex.

A string of questions starts swirling around in my head, shattering everything that was so organized into a million pieces. What is he doing here? Why did he show up all of a sudden, after so long?

"Hi, Henrique."

His voice is deep and makes my pulse quicken. I remember him whispering in my ear and the days when he said we would be together forever. I feel my legs give way when he smiles and gets up to hug me. I let him wrap me in his now-stronger arms, and I know that he can feel my wild heartbeat. I revert to that eighteen-year-old from before the test results, dreaming about spending the rest of my life with someone and thinking everything was falling into the right place.

"Hi" is all I manage.

"I'll let the two of you talk," Eric says in a voice that couldn't be further from his usual good mood. He doesn't like Carlos but seems so shocked that his neurons still haven't had time to activate his full irony mode. Instead, he acts polite. "Can I get you anything, Carlos? Water, coffee?"

"No, man, thanks," he answers, finally letting go of me and waving when Eric disappears into his bedroom. Then Eric comes back and walks quickly across the living room and out of the apartment, because he must think it's not a good idea to be in the same environment as my ex and me. Not after all this time, not after all the wounds that can easily be reopened with a simple conversation.

"What are you doing here?" I ask. Not curtly but curiously. My stomach growls again, more out of nervousness than hunger now.

"How is Eric doing?" asks Carlos without answering. I almost let out a laugh. If Kafka came down from the ceiling as a cockroach, it wouldn't be as weird as seeing Carlos here, as if we are best buddies who haven't seen each other in a couple of weeks. "Are those his wigs?"

"Yeah. He's been performing in drag shows."

"Cool," he says, his eyes squinting with his attractive grin.

I don't really know how to react. This is my home, my living room, yet I feel like the stranger here. I thought I had broken free of the power Carlos had over me, but he is still my first love, and I wonder about his reason for being here. About everything he's done and how he severed our connection so abruptly, to then return without even bothering to text first and ask if we could meet.

He knows I hate surprises.

"You haven't changed a bit, Henrique," he says, sitting back down on the chair and placing his hands on his knees.

"And you've changed a lot. Is that a new tattoo?" I say, pointing at his arm.

"Yeah! Do you like it? I got it in New Zealand."

And then the silence takes over the room when he realizes what he's just said. How happily he said it, as if leaving had been a wonderful decision. As if I'd been just a meaningless detail in the equation that is his life.

He looks away. I take a deep breath, trying to organize my thoughts.

"Did you like it there?" I decide to make conversation, to pretend like he's a neighbor I just ran into on the elevator and that we're making small talk about the clouds in the sky, how blazing hot the weather is, or how rude it is when people don't throw their trash down the chute, instead leaving the bags lying around in the hallways. "They say it's a beautiful place."

"Henrique . . . I didn't come here to talk about New Zealand."

He looks me in the eye, and I stare back. I want to turn away, I want to take him by the neck and strangle him, I want to scream and kick him out, but all I do is blink. I don't let it show how it affects me, as much as it does. If this were a play, I'd be Macbeth, ruthless and cold, nothing inside me to let him think he still holds any kind of power.

Even if he does. Even if, deep down, he still stirs me in a way I can't quite explain.

"What did you come here to talk about, then?" I ask, waiting for him to look away. And he does, at his flip-flops.

"About . . . the two of us."

He doesn't seem like the guy I fell in love with, who was so sure of himself. Instead, he seems to have been curbed by time, as if he's reverted to being a teenager, full of doubts about himself and expectations for the future.

"There's no *two of us*, Carlos. You ended any possibility of *two of us* when you ran away to New Zealand."

I swallow it: the tears, the anger at his lack of maturity, the impulse to tell him to go fuck himself and to never show his face here again, the urge to throw myself on him and kiss him, to rip off those clothes to see what his body looks like after all that sun. All I do is remain still, staring at him as if I were in charge of a totally out-of-control situation.

"I know, I . . . I panicked, okay?"

I shake my head and smirk. "Poor you," I say sarcastically. "I *was* panicked, too. I *was* panicking, and for a long time, all there was to do was to face what had to be faced. Not run away without looking back. By the way, how's your grandmother doing?" I ask with a smile.

"Stop that, Henrique." He knows that excuse wasn't the best lie in the world, but he doesn't even try to justify it. "I needed some time away from . . . from all of this. From all the drama and the things that weren't doing me any good. I was a completely different person from who I am today, and I needed to find myself. I was confused, afraid of what my parents would say if they found out I was gay. But now it's different!"

"So you came out to your parents?"

"I did," he says matter-of-factly. I have to admit, I'm more than a little surprised to learn this. "It was hard at first—really hard. But eventually my mom grew to accept it, and because of her, I think my dad has started to come around. It's not perfect, but it's better. And it's made me think about what I want in life, and what I want is to move on. With you."

"I'm happy for you, Carlos. Really, I am," I say, and I mean it. "But it's too late. I didn't have the luxury of running away from the drama and the things that didn't do me any good. I've never needed anyone as much as I needed you back then, and you disappeared without even a goodbye. You planned to disappear for eight months, and you didn't even have the guts to be honest with me. And now you come back as if nothing happened, after all this time? Why no phone call or text about what you were thinking? Why no warning about planning to go away and leave everything we'd built behind? And why would you come back now?"

"You may not believe it, Henrique, but I couldn't stop thinking about you during all the time I was away. I know I was an asshole and that I don't deserve anything from you—not your forgiveness or your trust—but time helped me digest everything that was happening and what my part was in your life. I had a kind of revelation, you know? I was in bed with a guy whose name I don't even remember, and I realized I was fucking miserable. It didn't matter that I was in Middle-earth or that I could open my window every day to the most beautiful view I'd ever seen in my life. I just wanted to come back. I was lonely; I had no one to talk to about the gorgeous things I saw every day. I tried to find someone, I swear I did, but no one was as good as you. So I realized I had to do this as soon as possible; I had to try to talk to you. I want to get back together, Henrique. I want to be in your life again, and to be by your side, no matter the risks I need to take to make that happen."

His narcissism knots my stomach: *He* was lonely, *he* wanted to get back together, *he* wanted to be a part of my life, *he* would make the sacrifice to be with me, *he* would take the risks, *he* wanted to run away. *He, he, he*. There was nothing in that mess of words that referred to *us*, nothing to make me see him with anything but a mix of curiosity and suspicion.

I can't believe anything he says. There's nothing he can say that will make me forget all the pain he caused and all the time I needed for the wounds to heal. The beauty I found so attractive is now nothing but the shell of someone who's ugly on the inside.

I grew up learning that the best way to move forward is not to stew in your anger but to forgive those who have done you harm. Even though I don't have a religion, certain Christian teachings are still rooted in me. But I've now learned that the philosophy behind them is true. I don't hate Carlos. I'm scared, mad, and surprised, but all these temporary feelings are here only because he showed up unannounced; they are nothing more than tall flames that, with time, will die out. I've come to realize that burning hatred that remains hot even through roaring winds is not a part of me anymore. Not like before.

"There's nothing between us anymore, Carlos," I say, feeling a peace that astonishes me. "We had our chance, and you let it escape."

He seems surprised and, in a way, offended.

"But you don't understand, Henrique. I came back for you! I want you back, whether you have HIV or not!"

I laugh, because he really does think everything boils down to what *he* wants.

"Of course I understand, Carlos. But in your calculations, you're forgetting to add something really important: what *I* want."

He blinks frenetically, as if that hadn't occurred to him yet. He opens and shuts his mouth, trying to articulate something, and a few seconds pass before he can say anything.

"You found someone, didn't you?"

"That's irrelevant, Carlos."

He shakes his head and frowns, disappointed. "That's exactly what it is. And that's so . . . unfair. I came back for you, Henrique. I don't care that you have HIV, I . . . I want to be with you."

"But I've moved on with my life, Carlos. I'm sure you'll find someone."

"No!" he yells, making me jump and shrink back. Tears well up in his eyes, and they're not sad but frustrated tears. His shoulders seem tense, his posture like that of a child who didn't get ice cream after a walk in the park, and the look on his face scares me. "You think I haven't tried to find someone? I want you, Henrique. Of all the people in the world, I am choosing you because you are the one I want. How hard can that be to understand?"

"It's not hard, but I also need you to understand that my wishes need to be fulfilled, and right now, I don't need you."

Carlos goes silent for almost half a minute, staring at me as if I were an alien. At last, he answers, his eyes downcast and his pride hurt. "I hope you understand the consequences of your choice, Henrique. You'll never find someone who'll make you as happy as I can."

"Only time will tell," I answer, getting up from the couch and walking to the front door. "I don't think we have anything left to say to each other, Carlos."

He gets up with a weight on his shoulders, but before he walks through the door and out of my apartment, he looks me in the eye, and I notice that there is something there, something beyond his hurt pride or disbelief, something . . . different. Something I've only seen once in my life, when I stared into my mother's eyes when I left home.

"You're going to regret this," he mutters, and I feel a chill down my spine, because that was the exact same sentence my mother said to me. The same words, the same tone of voice, the same cold, spiteful eyes.

Carlos leaves, and I try not to worry. My mom was wrong. I've never regretted leaving her house, not for one second. I also won't regret that I—finally—got rid of the person who was once the biggest love of my life.

# CHAPTER 19

# IAN

IT'S IMPOSSIBLE TO GET VANESSA to calm down in the days leading up to her college entrance exam. She paces around the house, always with an open book in front of her, like an actress about to play Isolde who still hasn't memorized any of the lines. She eats breakfast, lunch, and dinner with those books. And when she's too tired of the weight of the pages full of infographics of cells and nervous and digestive systems, she grabs her tablet and puts in earbuds, then watches videos about biomedicine for university students. I have no idea how she's able to understand all the bizarre eight-syllable terms.

"Vanessa, calm down!" I say, sitting at the dining room table and trying to stand my ground. Mom's blueprints have almost taken over the table, and I'm scribbling some calculations for a microeconomics assignment. "Everything is going to be fine!"

"Stop disturbing me!" she says, scratching her head under her thick hair, closing her eyes, and slamming a fist against her forehead. "RNA: ribonucleic acid; controls the synthesis of proteins in cells. DNA: deoxyribonucleic acid; holds the necessary information for the construction of RNA proteins. Nucleotides: building blocks of nucleic acids formed by the esterification of phosphoric acid nucleosides. Esterification—"

"My God, Vanessa, you're going to work yourself to death!" I yell. How she manages to keep all these terms straight is a mystery I'll never unravel.

"I know, I know!" She throws the book on the couch and proceeds to let herself fall to the floor in a dramatic gesture, her legs and arms open and her stomach up, like the *Vitruvian Man*. "I'm gonna lose my mind. I'll never get into college and will spend the rest of my life selling fake jewelry in Copacabana. Do you think if I make some DNA necklaces, people would buy them?"

I can't help but laugh. I close my notebook, then walk to where she is and offer my hand. Vanessa eyes me for a few seconds, makes a dramatic sound from the back of her throat—something like "Uhhhnnn I don't waaant to get uuup"—but finally accepts my help and takes my hand. Her body is light, and she yelps when I pull her hard, making her get up quickly.

"The test is this weekend, Ian," she mumbles, grabbing the book again and placing it on her lap as she sits on the couch. "It's Thursday. I know nothing. I'll never get in."

"Of course you will. You just said a bunch of super-hard

biology terms without even looking at the book, and for a moment it seemed like you were actually studying for the last semester of med school. You got this."

"But it's so hard!"

"Of course it is. And if you don't get in, there's always next year. Or other options!" I say, trying to get her to realize that not going to college is a valid alternative.

"No! There are no other options!" she answers, unyielding, and picks up the list of terms from where she stopped. "Esterification: chemical reaction in which a carboxylic acid reacts with an alcohol, producing ester and water. Carboxylic acid: organic oxyacid that contains a carboxyl group. Carboxyl—"

"Dear Lord!" I decide to give up on trying to convince Vanessa to slow down, and join her instead.

I go to the kitchen and make some coffee for the two of us, since I also need to finish my microeconomics project, as it's half my final grade. I make some extra, because I know this family runs on caffeine, and it's likely that everyone will want some, even though it's almost ten p.m.

While the coffee maker whirs and wafts the delicious smell of hot water mixed with ground coffee, my phone beeps with a new text. From Gabriel.

Gabriel:

You busy?

Just another day trying to survive in this zoo
I call home.

Gabriel:

LOL. I'll call. I have news.

The phone rings right away.

"Guess what?" asks Gabriel, without even saying hi.

"You won the lottery?"

"No."

"The last pig you inseminated gave birth to a cow?"

"No."

"Okay, I give up."

"May eighteenth."

"What?"

"May eighteenth," Gabriel repeats. "Save the date."

"Why?"

"Because you're going to be my best man."

"What?"

"Daniela said yes, man! I asked and she said yes, and now it's official: We're engaged and have a date to get married. May eighteenth, after the two of us have graduated."

"Hold on, hold on— When did *that* happen?" I ask, surprised by the sudden information. "Last time you talked about Daniela, you told me you didn't know if you were ready for the next step, and now . . . now you're getting married? Since when have you been planning on asking her to marry you?"

"Right? I'm as surprised as you are! I kind of just asked her, actually. It was all so sudden. You're the first person I'm telling this to."

"Why didn't you tell me you were planning this?! Gosh, that's great news, but . . . I thought you and Daniela were just . . . temporary, you know?"

"I didn't plan it! I just saw a freaking ring at a mall and thought it was perfect for her, and then one thing led to another and— Oh my God, what have I done?"

He seems as surprised as I am, as if he is having a Great Revelation at this precise moment. Or a stroke.

"Gabriel?" I ask when the phone goes silent and all I can hear is his loud breathing.

"Hold on." I hear him pressing something on the phone and then placing it somewhere. "There, you're on speaker. I need a drink."

I hear his footsteps, a cabinet opening and closing, and the clink of a glass by the phone. He's probably having a shot of whiskey, like one of those tycoons in American TV shows who needs something strong to help him relax.

"I proposed to Daniela."

"Have you calmed down?" I ask, not quite knowing what to say or how to give him advice in case he reaches the conclusion that it probably wasn't the best idea he's ever had.

"I proposed to Daniela," he repeats. "Fuck."

"Yeah. Can you imagine how jealous Vanessa is going to be?"

He croaks a laugh. "I love Daniela," he says, and I hear more liquid being poured, the clinking of ice against glass, and the noise of a throat gulping whiskey very quickly. It must be whiskey. He'd never drink wine to try and calm down. Or even beer.

"It sounds like you did the right thing. Do you regret it?"

"Not at all."

"Okay, well, that's good. That's great. No regret is the best thing to feel when you make such a decision," I say to encourage him.

"Yes. It was an impulsive decision, but a good one. It was the right one. Was it the right one?"

"Of course it was!" I say reassuringly. "You love her, and even though I don't know her that well, I know you were made for each other. And that's all there is to it." That's the best supportive speech I can come up with on such short notice.

"You're going to be my best man, right?"

"Of course I am!"

"And who's going to be my second-best man?"

"Second-best man?" I ask. "What do you mean?"

"It's custom that your best friend's boyfriend also gets to come to the wedding, right? I don't know how these things work, but that's what it's like in the movies, so that's how this is going to be. So, who's my second-best man?"

"I think you should get yourself a bridesmaid, my friend, because things aren't really going anywhere around here. My only boyfriend right now is Hal."

"Hal?"

"Hal Varian, who wrote *Microeconomics: A Modern Approach*."

"Ugh."

"Yeah."

"And how are things in your life?" he asks, relaxing, thanks to either the whiskey or the change of topic. I know that when he says *your life*, he means the meds, the HIV, and the new routine. I smile. I love knowing he cares.

"All right" is my summary, because that's more or less the truth.

"No crises?"

"A different one every day, but I can now deal with all of it without complications. People say it gets better, but we can only really believe that when we start living one day at a time."

"That's really good to hear, Ian. It really is." Gabriel takes a deep breath. "I hope one day HIV will be only a footnote in a life full of good stuff and nice people."

"It will," I answer.

I'm about to start asking about Gabriel's schoolwork and how long until he has to defend his thesis, but I'm interrupted by a ripping sound followed by the clatter of a million books falling on my bedroom floor. Vanessa's voice comes next in a string of curses that I never thought I'd hear from such a small mouth.

I go to the bedroom and see that the bottom of her backpack is torn, and at least eight dictionary-sized books are scattered around the floor. She's still cursing, grabbing each one and tossing it on her bed, and then she proceeds to kick the ball of frayed fabric that her backpack has become.

"Vanessa is a bit worked up because the exam is this weekend,"

I say to Gabriel, who has gone completely silent and must be curious about the string of curse words on my side. "I have to go."

"I'll text her, but tell her I'm sending positive vibes."

"I will."

I hang up the phone and start helping my sister pick up the books from the floor. She's sitting on her bed with a physiology textbook she borrowed from her school library, her eyes a little empty, staring at a random spot on the wall.

"Vanessa, you need to get some rest."

"I need to study," she whispers back, then clears her throat and takes a deep breath. "My God, I am so tired."

I yank the book out of her hands and put it back with the others, then grab them two by two and place them on the table. I turn on the TV, go to Netflix, and start the next episode of *Grey's Anatomy*, which she's stopped watching.

"You have to be less like Cristina Yang, Vanessa," I say as she sees the episode. Watching this show was always her compromise to let herself stop studying yet still continue to be immersed in the world of medicine. Little by little, I found myself watching with her and becoming invested in these fictional characters. "Come on, let's watch this."

"I don't have a backpack to use for school tomorrow."

"You can use mine. Just take out my books and leave them on the table."

"How will you take your things to class?"

"I'll put two pens in my pocket and grab a piece of paper from someone; that's all I really need." She rests her head on my lap, and while we follow the dramatic lives of Meredith, Bailey, and Cristina, she closes her eyes and falls asleep immediately.

+

After my microeconomics class on Friday morning, I decide to kill some time at the mall. The Rio de Janeiro heat is unbearable, and the air-conditioning in that mecca of brand names and unnecessary products is very attractive.

I go to the bookstore and leaf through some books, thinking about buying one but reach the conclusion that I won't have time to read it. I go to the movie theater to see if there's anything good playing and end up buying a ticket for a Disney cartoon starting in a half hour. I don't have much to do, so I go to Starbucks for a coffee, find a seat, and wait for them to call my name.

It's one of those rare moments when I'm not thinking of anything bad. I think about my finals, about what might have happened between Henrique and Victor, about Vanessa's stress over her exam, and about what's in store for Gabriel and Daniela, but I don't really think of the bad things that have been going through my mind recently. I don't think of medicine or defense cells, viral load or blood tests. In that gap when I'm thinking about my coffee, I'm just a normal guy, killing time until I catch a movie, who—even though he is currently alone—doesn't feel lonely. I'm comfortable in the soft chair, staring at the menu attached to the wall with its Refreshers, brownies, and cupcakes. I watch the baristas move around with their cups and liquids and sweet syrups, all so concerned about being efficient that they barely have time to think about their own lives, their futures, and what happiness means to them.

"Ian?" I hear the barista call, and I pick up my coffee. I check the clock on my phone, and when I go back to my seat I'm suddenly aware of how crowded the place is, how everyone is talking over one another, and how the background music isn't really making the place feel more welcoming.

"Anyone sitting here?" a guy asks, and I shake my head. He smiles and sits in front of me, opens his backpack, and pulls out a book the size of a weightlifter's arm. It's a new copy, still shrink-wrapped, which he opens eagerly like a child tearing open a present.

I see the cover and can't help but laugh when I notice the title.
*Microeconomics: A Modern Approach* by Hal Varian.

"Some light reading to pass the time?" I say, starting a conversation. I'm not sure what makes me do it. I usually stay silent, preferring to listen to people's conversations around me as if I were one of those writers who likes to base their characters on the lives of strangers.

He looks up at me and smiles. "For how much this baby cost, it better be more exciting than *Game of Thrones*."

"A financial fight for the economic understanding of microenterprises, land production, commodities, and services," I say in the voice of a narrator, trying to sound dramatic. "The second half in particular is drenched in blood, sweat, and tears, with individual and market demands, elasticity, uncertainty, and the greatest villain of economics: the Slutsky equation."

"I heard macroeconomics is grander."

"Nonsense. That's for people who can't appreciate the

microcosm. It's like saying Lord of the Rings is better than *One Hundred Years of Solitude* just because it takes place on a continent instead of in a small village in rural Colombia."

"Whoa, a literary economist. And people say you can't meet anyone interesting at a coffee shop."

I'm a little embarrassed by the comment. Is he flirting with me? I take a better look at him. He's my age, maybe a little younger, since there's no hair on his face. He has thick black hair, hazel eyes, and tanned skin. He has a tattoo on his arm, mostly covered by his sleeve, and all I can see is the end of what looks to be a tribal pattern, or a key, or a turtle. Or a tribal pattern depicting a turtle with a key for a tail. Who knows.

"And you're a freshman," I say, trying to ignore the fact that he possibly and perhaps maybe definitely for sure just flirted with me. "That or you're really into Hal Varian."

"I start next semester. If I get in, that is. I should know in the next month or so."

"So you've already bought the book before you even know if you got into the program?"

"Yeah. It may sound strange, but it's a thing I do: Every time I try something new, I start thinking about what it would be like if I were already doing it, and I act accordingly. I was at the bookstore, saw the book, and thought, *Why not?*" He shrugs as I try to follow his unique reasoning. I've never heard anyone say anything like that.

"It's a little risky, isn't it? I mean, let's assume you don't get into that program. The book would be like a ghost tormenting you, reminding you that you didn't get in."

"I'm not that much of a pessimist. I have three heavy coats I bought before a trip to New York that I ended up not taking; two tickets to the Kaiser Chiefs concert in São Paulo, which I didn't attend; and three criminal law books from when I tried to get into law school last year and failed."

"That sounds a little . . ." I try to find a word that's not too mean, but I'm afraid he might take offense.

"Stupid? Idiotic? A waste of money?"

"Yeah."

"Everyone thinks so, but I don't mind." He smiles, and I see he really isn't offended. His smile narrows his long eyes to the point of almost closing them, and I'm sure his family is native Brazilian or Bolivian, or both. "We spend so much money on useless stuff. This is my useless stuff, and who knows if in the future it won't do me some good, even if I end up donating it to someone who needs it more than I do."

"Fair enough," I answer, checking my phone for the time. "But it still means you're the kind of person who has expectations about things that haven't happened yet, and that might not always work out so well."

I take a sip of my coffee and hear the barista yell, "Gustavo!" which makes him get up and walk to the counter. I assume he's not coming back, that he must be so offended by my attempt to psychoanalyze him after only a two-and-a-half-minute conversation, but he comes back and sits across from me, holding a green Frappuccino.

"They sell kale Frappuccino here?" I ask, curious.

213

"It's green tea," he answers. "I don't drink coffee."

That should be a crime, but I don't say anything.

"Right," he says, because my expression doesn't hide how surprised I am. "My mom almost disinherited me when I told her I don't like it. She said that Colombian children who don't drink coffee are as offensive as Americans who don't eat barbecue and don't believe in meritocracy. But the heart wants what the heart wants, and the stomach wants what the stomach wants. And mine has never wanted coffee."

"A valid point," I say, which provokes a smile. I check the time again.

"Are you late for an appointment?" he asks, meddling a little too much. "Or waiting for someone? Your girlfriend, maybe?"

I look at him with my best "You've got to be kidding me" face.

"Okay, fine. Boyfriend, then," he says, and then grins when he notices I don't take offense.

"A movie," I say. "I'm catching the next showing. By myself."

"If I had time, I'd go with you."

"And who says I'm not one of those guys who prefers to go to the movies alone?"

"It's a public place, so there'd be nothing you could do to stop me."

This time, I'm the one smiling. He's very forward.

"That doesn't mean we can't watch another movie some other time," he adds. He opens the backpack in his lap, grabs a pen from a pencil case, and scribbles something in his notebook. Then he rips the page, folds the paper in half, and hands it to me. "If you feel like it, text me. I also added my handle so you can find me on Instagram, in case you'd like to."

I grab the paper pinched between his index and middle fingers, not sure how a quick stop at Starbucks has resulted in me getting an interesting guy's phone number.

This has never happened to me before. It's almost as if the universe were throwing Gustavo at me. Not that I believe in fate, destiny, or any of that BS.

"Ah! Good luck with the program," I say before getting up.

"Thank you," he answers, then takes a sip of his green Frappuccino.

I shove the paper in my pocket and turn to walk away, thinking about how bizarre life can be, with all these coincidences that happen without warning, and that being in the right place at the right time is the kind of luck that doesn't happen that often.

And then reality hits me: As much as I was in the right place at the right time, I still have doctors' appointments, still have to worry about my viral load and my CD4 count, still have to get regular blood tests, and still have to take my medicine every day.

I still have HIV, and the fact that it's as real as the interest that boy showed in me makes me think nothing will ever work out.

# CHAPTER 20

# VICTOR

MY MOM STILL WON'T LET the twins use the internet, but she's not home and my dad is taking care of everything, so of course they're glued to the TV and the computer, shouting, "BLOW UP!" and "GUN THEM DOWN, DAMMIT!" Luckily, I'm in my room and their screams are muffled by my headphones.

I stare at my notebook and try to come up with the structure of what might become the script for the short film for my video production class. We don't have to shoot anything, but the instructions made it clear that the script needs to be financially viable for independent production and no more than eight pages, which means it should be between five and seven minutes long.

My first idea was to make a silent film about a romance between two guys: grayscale, title cards, exaggerated expressions, and a happy ending. At first, it seemed like a good story, but it obviously triggered my memory of Henrique, so I scrapped the idea.

I then thought of writing a drama about a boy who's separated from his mother and sets off to try and find her. But that's been overdone, and I couldn't forget about all the problems Henrique has faced with his mom.

The third idea was about a girl who walks around town and discovers no one is talking to her because she has white hair, while everyone else has black hair. It's not very original, but at least it doesn't make me think about Henrique.

I start typing out the premise: what the girl will look like, what the city where she walks is like, what she thinks, what she's going to say (if she ends up saying anything at all), how many characters are going to walk by her, what they represent, how to make it all flow and seem natural, what the outcome will be, and how I'm going to fit all of this into a maximum of eight pages.

I feel someone grab my shoulder, and I turn around, startled, taking off my headphones. It's my dad, looking at me with a concerned expression, probably because I've been staring at the blank Word document for at least ten minutes after I wrote down the first few words, and I haven't even noticed it.

"Is everything okay, son?" he asks, putting a coffee mug next to my computer. "Here, you need it more than I do."

"Thank you," I answer. "I'm thinking."

"Of what?"

*Henrique*, I want to say.

"The final assignment for one of my classes."

"Do you need help?" My dad has always thought of himself as a frustrated writer, with two finished crime novels sitting in his drawer that have never seen the light of day (and that aren't even half-bad, by the way) about an investigator who uncovers murders in a small town in a rural part of Brazil.

"SON OF A BITCH!" Caíque shouts, and my dad yells, "HEY, WATCH YOUR MOUTH!" over the sound muffling my younger brother's ears, prompting him to look up and mutter an apology.

My dad isn't exactly the figure of authority in our home, which makes everything seem like it's about to collapse when my mom is out. I'm used to it by now, but it's always funny to see him almost panic when he needs to deal with Raí and Caíque. I think he must have spent many sleepless nights wondering if it was a good idea to have more kids after I was already old enough to be independent, because the plan was to have just one more child, not the restless and rowdy duo he and my mom got.

"It's okay, Dad," I answer, drinking the (horrible!) coffee he made.

He smiles and watches me from behind the thick lenses of his glasses. His expression betrays his fatigue from all the yelling throughout the evening, as well as the accumulated exhaustion from his shifts at the hospital. I'm still happy he's trying to dedicate whatever sliver of energy he has to helping me.

"Actually . . ." I start, and I can see the excitement in his eyes. "I need to write a script for my video production class, and I was thinking of doing a sci-fi short about a girl who's different and is hated by everyone just because of that."

So I explain the concept, and he listens to everything, interrupting me once in a while to ask a question: "What are this girl's parents like?" "Is she from a family where everyone is different, or is she different from her loved ones, too?" "How is her relationship with older people?" etc., etc. At some point, the protagonist becomes fully formed in my head, and she is much more three-dimensional than the eight pages of script will allow me to demonstrate.

After a few minutes of talking, my dad runs to the living room to take care of some crisis between the twins, who've started screaming at each other and breaking things, and I continue to stare at the Word document, now with a few more words in it. And I surprise myself when I think of how lucky I am for having the parents I have.

I take my eyes off the computer screen and can see the top of my blue hair reflected in the mirror in front of me, and I think about how my mom and dad's first reactions when they saw it were a big laugh and a bunch of comments about how I looked like Sadness from *Inside Out*. There was no scolding, no threat of shaving my head if I didn't fit the standards that the neighbors and the rest of the family considered normal, not even that look that conveys much more than words can say. They just laughed, asked if the hairdresser did other colors as well, and moved on to setting the dinner table.

I've never had one of those big, embarrassing "Let's have a serious conversation" moments with my family, so I don't know what that's like in the grand scheme of things, because everything here has simply just always followed its natural course, like a warm stream in a cold ocean. I've never had to interrupt dinner to say, "I have something to tell you: I'm gay." Maybe that's because I've always learned that I shouldn't hide who I am or look differently at people who aren't like me.

I remember asking my dad when I was only eight if it was a problem that I thought a boy in school was good-looking, because all the boys in my class said it was wrong and that since I was a boy, I should be paying attention to girls. I thought they were pretty, too, I'd said, but I wasn't interested in them. Back then, I didn't know anything about life, but I remember my dad telling me that I could see beauty in whomever I wanted. And I also noticed there was something in his eyes, something I'd never seen before and that—in the confused mind of a child—might very well have looked like disappointment. But it was nothing like that. The look was of love and most of all concern. My dad knew the world was not exactly what he pictured and that other people didn't always think like him. And I'm almost sure that he knew, right there in that moment, just how different I was—how I wasn't the boy he'd imagined I would be or wished I would become. And then the look changed, and he smiled, and I noticed that beyond the worry, the disappointment, or the fear, he saw in me the most beautiful person in the world.

And that is why every time I hear someone describe their family problems, their issues with sexuality, or how hard it is to come out of the closet, my first reaction is to listen. I listen because I don't know what that's like, and I don't want to belittle the pain and suffering of people whose realities are so different from mine. I listen because I learned from a young age that empathy starts when we learn to put ourselves in other people's shoes, especially when they are so unlike us.

I realize, looking at the reflection of the small streak of blue hair, how hard my parents have tried to remain a part of my life without invading the space that I have to make my own decisions. It's bizarre to think that I can actually count on them when I need some advice, be it about a script for film school or about what I need to do to move forward with my life.

"Dad?" I call, when I realize the crisis in the living room is under control.

He pokes his head into my room and asks what I want.

"Can I talk to you?"

He raises an eyebrow and walks into the bedroom, leaving the door ajar in case the twins decide to have another round.

"Why is it that I suddenly feel a heaviness in the air?" he asks, sitting on my bed while I close the laptop. "You're not about to tell me you're quitting school, are you?"

"That's not what it is!"

"Okay. You're not moving out, are you? Because I don't have a single buck in my savings account to help you rent a new place."

"No! Jeez, can you listen to what I have to say?"

"Okay." He interlaces his fingers impatiently. "You didn't become straight, right?"

"Dad!"

"Okay, okay. You talk."

"How do you undo some crap you did and then regretted, after you've already tried everything to make it right?"

He listens to my question but doesn't seem to take it in, because he keeps staring at me for a long time. I can see the gears in his head at work, slowly at first, then quickly. I can almost see the smoke coming out of his ears.

"You've become a drug dealer, haven't you?"

"Oh my God, Dad! I don't do anything stronger than coffee!"

"Okay, so you're gonna have to help me and be a little more specific, because I'm going crazy with all the possibilities here."

"First of all, it's nothing illegal," I say with a sigh and an involuntary eye roll. Then I remember how Sandra always tells me that rolling my eyes is a quirk, and so I focus them. "It's just . . . there's this guy . . ."

"Oh, yeah. A guy," he mumbles, sounding very interested.

"Yes, a guy. And I really like him, and I'm sure he likes me. But I screwed up, and I don't know how to fix it, because now he won't look me in the eye anymore." My dad still seems concerned, looking at me as if I were spelling out all the decimal points of pi. "This is weird, isn't it? Asking my dad for advice about boys?"

"Maybe not exactly common practice, but our family is not well known for its normalcy," he comments. "I might not have a lot of experience in the boy department, but I have experience with human beings, and that's enough. I mean, I work with people of all kinds at the hospital, and if you knew the stories I hear . . . But anyway, boys. Gee, that's complicated. You've already apologized to him, yeah?"

"In all kinds of ways."

"And did he listen to you?"

"He did, and he said he forgave me but also that he didn't want anything to do with me anymore."

"That's not forgiving, if he really likes you."

"I know, but now I can't think of anything else I can do to try and redeem myself."

"On a scale of stealing a loaf of bread to embezzling public health-care funds, what level of screwing up are we talking about here?"

"I embezzled the health-care money to buy bread, Dad," I answer, and he nods, astonished. "That's how bad I screwed up."

"Okay, well, that's not good."

"No, it's not. Any advice?"

He thinks for a moment, staring at the blue streak in my hair.

"The first thing we ask for when a patient walks into the emergency room is for them to calm down. We say we'll do everything we can to help them walk out as healthy as possible. That helps a little, so I think that's the best advice I can give you: Calm down. Maybe this guy is just a disappointment and in two or three months you won't even remember him. Or maybe he's one of those unforgettable people, but only time will tell. But in my opinion, if you think he really likes you the way you like him, things will work out and fall into the right place, because that's more or less what tends to happen."

I don't know if that's good advice, but I think it's all my dad can come up with on the spot. I smile when I see that he feels awkward discussing boys with his eldest son but still does it without judgment. So I hug him, and he hugs me back.

"And please don't become a drug dealer. Or straight. That would be really confusing to me."

"You got it, Dad," I say, letting go of him with a smile.

We hear the doorbell, louder than the screams of the twins, and my dad frowns because we're not expecting anyone on a Friday evening. He walks out of the bedroom to see who it is, and I again focus on my script.

I hear the bedroom door fly open, and Sandra bursts in like a hurricane, her hair held in a loose knot by a ballpoint pen. Her face is puffy, like someone who just got out of bed, and she's wearing the Powerpuff Girls pajamas she'd never wear outside unless it was a real emergency, even if she's my next-door neighbor and we don't have to take more than twenty steps between our bedrooms.

She's breathless, as if she just walked up eighteen flights of stairs in less than two minutes. I notice her eyes are wide, her mouth is contorted in dread, and her phone is lit up in her hand.

"Sandra? What happened?"

"Instagram. Did you see it?" she asks, staring at me as if war had just broken out and I'd been recruited to the front lines.

"N-no," I say, immediately opening the app and accessing my profile.

"Film group." She hands me the phone, and I feel a chill down my spine when I see Henrique's picture on a post. It's a montage, and there's a bloodred stamp over it with the cruel words:

# INFECTED WITH AIDS

What is a picture of Henrique doing on my school's film course group?

I realize the picture was shared by one of the students in our class, and it says:

Guys, check out this absurd thing I found in my feed! We gotta report this profile!!! He can't expose someone like this and walk away! What can we do to help this guy?! Fuck, man, I feel awful just reading this. Imagine how the guy in the picture must be feeling. This can destroy his life, right? Isn't this a crime? Please, if anyone knows how to help, just tell me in the comments! I've already reported this shithead's profile, but if everyone reports it, Instagram will take it down more quickly!!!

I feel my stomach churn when I read the caption under Henrique's photo. It's a selfie on top of the Corcovado: a picture of him smiling, sticking his tongue out, and winking, Rio de Janeiro behind him in all its glory.

**AIDS KILLS!!!**
5 HOURS AGO

So you think you know people, yeah????? You think you know who they are and you're sure that because they're pleasant and kind, they aren't DIRTY and ROTTEN on the inside? That they're not PROMISCUOUS and having sex with EVERYONE THEY SEE IN FRONT OF THEM?

This is an alert to everyone who thinks they know the people around them: YOU DON'T! AIDS is a disease that kills every day, and it has no cure and no face. Your best friend, your neighbor, or YOUR BOYFRIEND might have AIDS, and you'll never know. Case in point, the boy in this photo. Who would have thought that behind this innocent smile lurks A FILTHY DISEASE? I didn't know, but now I do, and it's my duty to tell this to everyone who wants to hear: He is INFECTED WITH AIDS!

Be careful when you meet him, because I'm sure he gives this DAMN DISEASE to everyone who has relationships with him.

Stay away! Be careful!

God loves all of you!

## CHAPTER 21

# HENRIQUE

IT'S MY WORST NIGHTMARE.

By the time I saw the post, my phone already had 145 messages, 35 missed calls, and 18 voice mails. My Instagram inbox had messages from 83 of my followers and message requests from 215 people I don't even know.

Message request from **Andrea Gomes**:
IT'S BECAUSE OF PEOPLE LIKE YOU THAT THIS WORLD IS LOST. JESUS IS COMING BACK TO END ALL OF YOU FILTHY GROSS PROMISCUOUS SOD-OMITES. LEVITICUS 20:13: IF A MAN ALSO LIE WITH MANKIND, AS HE LIETH WITH A WOMAN, BOTH OF THEM HAVE COMMITTED AN ABOMINATION: THEY

SHALL SURELY BE PUT TO DEATH; THEIR BLOOD SHALL BE UPON THEM. I HOPE THAT YOU WILL NOW UNDERSTAND THE WRATH OF GOD WITH THIS DISGUSTING DISEASE AND THAT YOU WILL DIE FAST BEFORE YOU INFECT INNOCENT PEOPLE. YOU SCUM!

Message request from **Humberto Fraga**:

Hey, Henrique, I don't know you and you don't know me, but I hope you find the strength to get through this. What this guy did is a crime, and you can report it. I am a social worker for a nonprofit organization for HIV-positive people and understand wanting discretion, with all the prejudice; I am positive myself and won't discuss my status with anyone due to family issues. Everyone has a right to discuss their status or not. If you need anything, you can message me, I will be happy to help. Have a good weekend!

Message request from **André da Silva**:

lmao infected with aids, you'll die cause you were a sucker, stupid fag.

▶ Audio (Mom):

"Henrique? What the hell is this story going around on the internet? You have AIDS? Since when have you known that and why would you not tell me? I'm your mother! I couldn't believe it when I saw it, but I am not surprised—you ended your life the moment you turned your back on your family and decided to embarrass us all. Are you aware of the consequences of your actions? How do you think I'm going to show my face outside now, when the news gets out into the neighborhood and everyone knows you're nothing but a degenerate?"

Ian Gonçalves:

Henrique, what happened? I saw the post, and I know it's a bunch of lies! How are you doing? Please send me a message when you can. If I can help with anything, just let me know.

Denise Machado:

Henrique, we're having a busy day at the office, and even though you aren't on the schedule, I want you to come in so we can talk. I'll see you at 1:00 p.m.

Message request from AIDS KILLS!!!:
I TOLD YOU YOU WERE GOING TO REGRET IT.

Carlos. I can't believe he dared to expose me in this way. How could someone be so selfish? As if that weren't enough, I'm immersed in a total black hole of toxic messages from people I don't know, even though none of them will make a difference in my life. With every positive message, I get the feeling that the world might not be such an awful place; but I'm only human, and

I end up focusing on the bad ones. Each one feels like a lit fuse crawling under my skin, burning slowly, and there is no way to put them out or make them stop.

All of a sudden, my world is upside down. The shares keep multiplying like the heads of a Hydra as more people see my face and draw their own conclusions. Some accuse me of "stealthing," a slang term for when someone goes around infecting other people on purpose; others tell me I need to let God into my heart; others tell me this is divine punishment for being gay, that it was never a question of if, but when. There's just so much hate. So much unprovoked hatred for someone with whom these people have never exchanged a single word in their lives. It terrifies me, how much hate can accumulate and explode on a computer screen.

"Stop it!" Eric rips the phone from my hand and locks the screen as soon as he catches me with my eyes fixed on it, my nervous fingers scrolling through the messages that never stop coming. "It's not doing you any good."

"Denise called me into the office," I answer. "She's going to fire me."

"She can't do that. If she did, she'd be committing a crime."

"She's going to fire me," I repeat. "And I'll never get another job again. And I can't even go back to living with my parents, because, according to my mom, I'm a degenerate who embarrasses her."

"Things will get better, Henrique," Eric says. That old saying every out gay person tells those who have just come out, and that's exactly how I feel—as if I've just come out one more fucking time. "You know it always gets worse before it gets better."

I sigh wearily, rubbing my face with my palms and trying to think clearly. "I just wish it would stop getting worse once and for all."

"What are you going to do about Carlos?" Eric asks, because it's an unavoidable question. I don't want to think about that bastard right now, but he's to blame for this weird onslaught of hate.

"I don't know," I answer, because that's the truth. I've never been this confused in my entire life. I know I can sue him, gather all the evidence and witnesses and start a case with the help of one of the organizations that messaged me. Besides Humberto Fraga, three more got in touch, on top of five HIV-support activists. But the whole legal issue is the least of my worries. A lawsuit can drag on for years in court, and Carlos could just disappear again, since that's his specialty. And even if I screw up his life, nothing will erase what I'm reading right now, the stream of judgment still piling up in my inbox. Nothing will assuage this perception I now have that our society is totally messed up. "Could we *not* talk about that asshole?"

In any other situation, Eric would insist we needed to talk about Carlos. But something about the look on my face—despair, fear, weariness, annoyance—makes him change his mind, and he just nods.

I check the clock and see it's almost noon.

"I need to get ready to go to the office." I get up from the couch, then walk to Eric and put out my hand. "I need my phone."

"Want me to come with you?" he asks.

"No. I need to be by myself." I reach out, and he gives me a doubtful look.

"I'll only give it back if you swear you'll stop reading those stupid comments."

"You got it."

He returns the phone, and I take it to the bathroom, and I play a Twisted Sister song as soon as I lock the door. I turn on the shower and sit on the toilet, still fully clothed, and keep reading the comments.

I can't stop myself.

+

The ad agency where I work isn't too far from my apartment, which means I can take the bus or the subway. Since it's a Saturday and there aren't as many people as on weekdays, I choose the latter, taking refuge underground, my headphones in my ears, eyes on the floor. Strangely, I'm scared that the posts will go from hate propagated by fiber-optic cables into a real-life manifestation. What if someone recognizes me? What if someone stops me, beats me up, calls me names? It feels like there's a bull's-eye printed on my back, like I'm on one of those wanted posters that you see in cowboy movies:

# HENRIQUE ANDRADE

### ACCUSED OF HAVING UNPROTECTED SEX AND CONTRACTING HIV
### REWARD: 10 MILLION DOLLARS IN GOLD BARS
### WORTH MORE THAN CASH!

When I buy my subway ticket, I notice that the subway traffic is a little more intense than usual, and I'm reminded that college entrance exams are this weekend. I ignore the parents coming back from the testing centers, discussing the heat or how anxious their kids are, and I sit in a corner of the ice-cold car, willing the trip to end quickly.

I get off the train and walk up the stairs, then walk to the building where my office is. I ignore the drowsy heat and how there seems to be no breeze this afternoon, as well as the street sellers offering knickknacks and men yelling, "Water! Soda! Beer!" as if they were selling tickets to paradise.

I walk into the elevator of the building and start sweating. It's impossible for me to convince myself that I should remain calm. My heart is beating fast, my palms are sticky, and my forehead is shiny with sweat. My body feels hot, the elevator is stuffy, and I'm sure I'm going to walk out of this place without the slightest clue how I'm going to pay my bills after I'm fired and the unemployment benefits have run out.

Today there are only eight employees at the agency out of the fifteen who usually crowd the open-plan and computer-filled office space. When I open the door to the agency, everyone stares at me. They all know, but they immediately go back to their computer screens. They whisper among themselves and exchange looks, and I notice that the air suddenly gets heavier. I want to cry. I want to walk out of this place and disappear forever. I don't want to have to face Denise and hear what she has to tell me. She's going to fire me and there's nothing I can do about it. She'll find an excuse, pressure me into not reporting her—anything to keep her company clear of any scandal.

"Henrique . . . is everything okay?" Alessandra, the receptionist, asks me. I'm sure she knows. Everyone already knows; they work for an ad agency, spend their whole days online. Of course they've seen the post!

"No," I answer dryly, which startles her, since I'm usually in a good mood or, when I don't feel particularly patient, am at least very polite. "Is Denise in her office?"

"Yes," she answers, taking the phone and calling her office. *She knows everyone is looking at me, watching me, judging me, avoiding me.* "Denise? Henrique is here." The receptionist nods, hangs up, and says I can go in.

Jonas is tossing one of those antistress massage balls up and down as he waits for the computer to finish rendering a video. Livia is focused on drawing something on her tablet, staring at the screen as if any mistake made can't be undone. In the back, I can see Denise behind the glass door of her office. She's typing furiously on her computer, completely focused.

As I walk by the desks toward my boss's office, I can feel sidelong glances (*They know, they're shaking their heads, they're turning around, they're judging me*), but everyone nods and smiles when I walk by, as if nothing has happened.

"What are you doing here, Henrique?" asks Jonas, scratching his head.

I shrug. "Denise wants to talk to me," I say, not slowing down, staring straight at my boss on the other side of the glass door. She raises her eyes and looks at me, then makes a gesture for me to come in.

I take a deep breath, knowing that a Saturday afternoon conversation can't be a good thing.

She's about to fire me.

"Henrique!" Denise is a thirtysomething-year-old with both arms covered in colorful tattoos, and she has an Afro with the tips dyed purple. Her red-rimmed glasses contrast with her pink lipstick, and there's a picture on her desk showing her hugging her five-year-old. "I'm sorry I texted you on a Saturday; I'm glad you saw it! Come over here, please."

I frown, going around her desk and wondering what her real intentions are. This is the moment she'll show me the post from last night and, with a heavy voice, explain why she can't have this kind of person at her company.

When I look at her computer screen, I don't see the post. Instead, it's the last image I edited for a cosmetics company.

"See this thing here?" she asks, pointing at the lips of two women, smiling side by side. "I sent it to the client and of course he requested a million changes, but the main one was the tone of the lipstick, because apparently they're selling, like, two hundred hues of red, and of course they didn't describe any of this in the contract for the ad. I would have asked Jonas to change the colors, but you're the best man for the job, and we need to make it as natural as possible. And Jonas is swamped with the videos for the Christmas campaign of that client who keeps asking for everything at the last minute and then for changes until the very last second." She takes a breath for the first time, as if she's only now remembered that her lungs actually need oxygen. She looks at me as if she doesn't pay me well enough to do this kind of thing. "You think you could get this fixed by three p.m., pretty please?"

I check my watch and see it's already one fifteen. If I start right away, I can do it.

"S-sure," I respond. "But what was the thing you wanted to talk about?"

Could she have missed that my personal life has been exposed all over the internet?

"Huh? This, obviously," she answers with a shrug. "Why do you think I'd make you come here on a Saturday unless it had something to do with work?"

I think about changing the subject, about giving her a tight smile and saying, "Okay, I'm gonna go fix the tones of the lipstick," but I change my mind. If Denise hasn't seen it yet, it's only a matter of time until she does. If everyone at the agency hasn't, and all the looks and whispers were just my wrong impression, it's only a matter of time before they become a reality and things start getting complicated.

"I thought you were going to bring up the post about me on Instagram," I say truthfully. "I have HIV—which is not the same as having AIDS—and I also don't go around giving it to other people. I'm on treatment, use condoms, and am undetectable."

I smile awkwardly, and when I look at her, she doesn't look like she's been caught by surprise. Denise straightens her glasses on her face, her shoulders raised by a long breath.

And that's when I realize she did see the post. Everyone at the agency has.

"Your personal life has nothing to do with your work,

Henrique," she tells me. "As long as you fulfill your duties and continue to be the great employee you've always been, I have nothing to say to you about any post. But if you have any issues in the company, please do not hesitate to let me know," she emphasizes. "I didn't create this agency to propagate prejudice or discrimination. We already suffer enough discrimination out there." She glances quickly at the photo with her son, and I know she's talking about everything she went through when she decided to adopt him despite being single. "This is a safe space."

I feel as if an electric current has stopped running through my body. Yes, everyone knows, everyone has seen the post, everyone is aware that I'm positive. But Denise is ready to make sure nothing will get to me. I can't go into the heads of any of my coworkers to find out what they're thinking. I don't know their prejudices, I don't know how they see life or difference, but, in this moment, I feel welcome, as if the bad things outside can't get me in here. My phone continues to vibrate with notifications, message requests from strangers, and texts, but I'm not thinking about those right now. Instead, I take my phone out of my pocket, press the off button, and walk to my desk, where I will edit an image and send it to the client in less than two hours.

+

I eat a flavorless burger at McDonald's and walk back home at almost four p.m. After I edited the photo, Denise told me to check another dozen small jobs, and I didn't say no to any of them because I knew that as long as I was immersed in those, it meant I didn't have to think about the real world.

But reality has this nasty habit of showing itself in the worst possible way, and that's exactly what happens when I round the corner toward my apartment.

Eric is turned to the wall, and I can see that there's a bucket near his feet with water and soap, and he's scrubbing the concrete with a cleaning brush. He turns around and sees me, and his expression changes from determined to sad in an instant, because he was there trying to protect me, to keep me from seeing the red spray paint on the wall:

# INFECTED WITH AIDS
## FAGGOT

# FILTHY          DISGUSTING

# DISEASED          SICK

But Eric is not alone. Next to him, I can see two other guys with sponges helping out. I see Ian's short hair and thick beard, gathering sweat, and Victor's slender body and blue streak of hair. They turn around, too, as soon as they see Eric has stopped scrubbing, and the three of them stare at me as the foaming water trickles down the wall in red hues, silently dripping on their shoes.

I walk toward them with a knot in my throat. I feel so much at the same time: sadness when I realize someone was capable of doing something this horrible; exhaustion with the thought that this might be just the beginning; dizziness because it's so hot. But most of all, I feel a tightness in my chest—a good one—because I know I have people around who are willing to protect me.

"I'm sorry, Henrique, I didn't want you to—"

Before Eric can finish, I grab the sponge from his hands and dunk it in the bucket, and with strong, constant strokes, I start washing off one of the words. Victor and Ian don't say anything; they just keep scrubbing as they look at me. They smile. And I smile back.

"Thank you" is all I can say before we go back to silence and pick up where they left off.

# CHAPTER 22

# IAN

EACH ONE OF THE SPRAY-PAINTED words on Henrique's wall feels like it is directed at me.

I feel a bitter taste in the back of my mouth when we're finally done cleaning the whole thing. When I saw what they posted about Henrique, I got in touch with Victor immediately. He told me Eric had called and told him someone had spray-painted something on the wall of their building, and he was going downstairs to erase it before Henrique had a chance to see it. I didn't think twice and offered to come along, and Victor gave me the address, telling me he'd be there in less than ten minutes.

There's still a pale pink shadow of the words on the concrete that will only be erased if someone gets a bucket of paint to cover it. Those words—still there even after all the soapy scrubbing—are a reminder that even if we try to erase what we don't want to see, there will always be something to remind us that fear and prejudice still exist.

"Thanks, guys," Henrique mutters, wiping the sweat from his brow and throwing the sponge back into the bucket. He has a distant look, his eyelids are heavy, and his shoulders are hunched, as if he's suddenly aged ten years in half an hour. He gives Victor a sideways look, and Victor smiles awkwardly but remains silent, staring at Henrique as if wanting to say something but not finding the courage to do it. "You want to come upstairs and grab something to drink?"

"You don't mind?" Victor asks, and I realize his shy words reveal something more than just a concern about invading Henrique's personal space.

Henrique smiles. "No."

We go upstairs, and Eric pours some iced tea into glasses before bringing them to us. We're sustaining an unpleasant silence, the type in which everyone feels like talking but no one dares say a word. I want to ask Henrique how he's doing, what he's thinking about, and who could have done something like this to him, but the words get caught in my throat.

As though he were reading my thoughts, Henrique says, "It's okay, guys. Thanks for the help with the wall, but you must be tired. Feel free to go home."

"Nothing is okay." That's Eric, and his voice makes it obvious that he's about to explode. "We need to do something, Henrique. He needs to pay for this."

"He?" I ask. "So you know who did it?"

Henrique, seeming exhausted, sits on the armchair and takes a sip of his tea. "It was my ex."

And then he tells us, briefly, about the conversation he had with Carlos and the threat he made before leaving the apartment.

Victor stares at him, his face a mask of uncontrollable rage. "That son of a bitch," he says as soon as Henrique is done. "Why would he do this?"

"Because I didn't take him back. And he must think that this way, no one else will ever want me."

"You know that's not true, Henrique," Victor says as soon as he notices the grief in Henrique's voice.

"I'm so . . . tired of it all." Henrique turns to Victor and looks at him, and I feel like this is not the best moment for Eric and me to be here, in this living room, watching the two of them stare at each other.

I want to get up and leave, but I remain still, not knowing what to do. Henrique's eyes are red again, but there are no tears. Just a weariness that seems to have been with him for many years and has finally shown itself. He lowers his head and sighs.

"Do you want to be by yourself?" Victor asks.

"No" is Henrique's immediate answer, and he tries to form a smile.

Victor gets up and walks to the armchair where Henrique is sitting. With a quick gesture, he brings Henrique's head to one of his shoulders, caressing his red hair with the tips of his fingers.

Henrique doesn't cry, but he closes his eyes and allows his head to be stroked. While they sit in silence, I grab my phone and check Instagram.

"The post was deleted," I say, confirming that the content shared throughout the day is no longer available. "And the profile that posted it doesn't exist anymore."

"That doesn't mean anything," Eric says. "We can still sue that asshole and make him pay for this."

"We're not doing anything." Henrique's voice is little more than a whisper. His eyes are still closed and his face seems a little more relaxed. "Leave it alone."

"Leave it alone? My dear, I'm a Scorpio rising and an Aries moon. I'll never just drop something like this!" Eric retorts, getting up from the armchair and collecting the glasses of tea.

"Do you think suing him will do any good?" Henrique seems skeptical. "All it's going to be is an even harder emotional strain, and he'll probably disappear from the face of the earth again. That's his specialty."

"All right, you don't want to sue the jerk, you have the right. Just like I have the right to bring him down, and that's exactly what I'm going to do."

It's impossible not to smile at Eric's exaggerations; he sounds excited and funny even in crappy situations like this one. I think he knows how much power he has, because the mood lightens immediately. Eric starts picking up around the house, and I follow him with my eyes while Henrique continues to rest from his rough day, eyes still closed.

"Here's the deal," Eric begins, slapping Henrique's leg and

making him open his eyes. "You know where this boy lives, don't you?"

"If he's back at his parents', of course I know," Henrique says. "Why?"

Eric sits on the floor, legs crossed, and he starts telling us what we're going to do. He's succinct and direct, but I get a sense of how amazing this could be. Or horribly stupid.

"No," Henrique says. "No, no, no, no, Eric, no way. You're not getting your friends involved in my problems. I don't want to have to deal with it anymore."

"But it's a great idea!" I chime in to support Eric.

I know I shouldn't meddle, but I can't help thinking of what I'd do if something like this happened to me. I can't stand to see someone like Carlos get away with it.

"We can't let the assholes of the world walk around as if there are no consequences, Henrique. And the girls would be happy to help, you know that," Eric says. When he notices Henrique is still shaking his head, he adds, "This is not up for discussion, my darling. You"—he points at the three of us—"have two options: You can either help or stay home. Either way, it will get done. All I need is his address."

"What if I say no?" Henrique asks.

"Are you really planning on saying no to a Scorpio rising with an Aries moon, my love?"

That's a real threat. Henrique lets out a brief laugh, which is a good sign. "Of course not. When are we doing it?"

We spend the next half hour going over the details of Eric's plan—Operation Rainbow, as he calls it—and Henrique's sadness is slowly replaced with excitement. We decide to put it into action this evening.

"Revenge is actually a dish best served hot!" says Eric, excited. He starts calling all the drag queens, making them cancel their party plans and telling them to get themselves ready at his place in about three hours.

I really want to stay with them, but I check the clock and see it's almost six p.m. I need to pick up Vanessa at the school where she's taking her college entrance exam. I tell them I'll just take her home and be back as soon as possible, because I'd never miss this evening's big event.

Victor, Eric, and Henrique continue to go over Operation Rainbow as I get ready to leave. I notice there's still something up in the air between Victor and Henrique. Eric, probably the most sensitive person in this apartment, has noticed it, too, and asks me to wait a moment while he gets changed. When Henrique shoots him a questioning look, Eric says he needs to buy all the ingredients necessary to, in his words, "create a rainbow" and declines Victor's and Henrique's offers to help, saying that the two of them should stay home and wait. He adds that Victor shouldn't leave because the more people who help, the better, and Eric even makes Victor call his best friend so she can come right away.

When Eric and I walk out of the apartment, I notice the conspiratorial smile on his face.

"You think they'll make up?" I ask as we go down the stairs and start saying goodbye.

"I'm sure they will," he says as he hugs me at the entrance. "If you're not back here by eight o'clock, I swear I'll do to you the same thing I'm about to do to Carlos."

"My dear, you're gonna need a Virgo to give some order to all this chaos you're about to create," I answer, smiling, and Eric raises an eyebrow. "What? Did you think *you* were the only one into astrology?"

"That's why I love Virgos. See you later!"

+

When I arrive to pick up Vanessa, she's already waiting for me outside, sitting on a low wall next to other students who are talking or waiting to go home. She looks tired, dangling her feet, her hands propped on either side of her body as she listens to something (probably classical music) on her headphones.

I wave as soon as I walk into her field of vision, and she offers a strained smile, removing her earbuds and giving me a tight hug that catches me by surprise, but I don't complain.

"So, what's up?" I ask. "How did the test go?"

"Who knows," she says in that nonchalant teenage way of talking about an important situation. "I just want to rest before tomorrow's exam session."

"Have you eaten anything?"

She shakes her head.

"Let's go eat, then."

We walk to a crowded diner, and I order two sandwiches. I see that Vanessa still has my backpack, since hers got ripped. There's a folded piece of paper in her hands, and she fiddles with it, passing it from her left hand to her right, and I notice her worried expression. At first, I think it's the result of today's exam, but when she hands it to me, I raise an eyebrow.

"I found this in your backpack, Ian. I'm sorry, I wish I hadn't seen it." She says it too quickly, without looking at me, staring at her feet. I see that her leg shakes up and down anxiously.

When I unfold the paper, the ends already crumpled and creased, I feel the world spin out of control.

It's my HIV quick test result.

I fold it again and put it in my pocket. Vanessa's eyes are filled with tears.

"I'm sorry," she mumbles, still not knowing what to do, what to say, how to react. "I shouldn't have opened it and intruded in your stuff."

She doesn't resent that I didn't tell her about it, and she's not looking at me differently. She's just concerned that she *intruded in my stuff.*

I reach across the table and take her hand. At first she pulls back, but I hold tight.

"Look at me, Vanessa," I say, and her eyes meet mine. I'm not worried about how many people there are in the diner, the hum of them walking by, or the staff at the counter screaming out order numbers for sandwiches. All I care about right now is my little sister and what is going through her head about these results. "Everything is okay."

She bites her lower lip, but I reach out with my other hand, now holding both of hers, confirming the words I just said.

Everything is okay.

Everything is okay.

Everything is okay.

"Everything is okay. For real," I repeat, holding her hands tighter and trying to make her feel comfortable.

"Do Mom and Dad know?"

"No. I don't know if I want them to," I say, and she nods.

"Have you told anyone?"

"Only Gabriel. And two other friends you don't know."

"And what did they say?"

"That I'd be an idiot if I thought for even one second that things between them and me would change for that reason." I let go of her hands when I hear someone shout our order number. I walk to the counter and pick up the tray with our sandwiches. "Are you mad at me?" I ask when I get back.

"Me? Why?"

"Because I didn't tell you anything."

"I'm happy that I know, because now I can tell you I'm here for whatever you need," she says in her natural voice, then grabs a fry and nibbles at it. "And no, I'm not mad at you."

I look away for a few seconds before answering. "Thank you."

"You don't have to thank me, Ian." She cleans her greasy hands to hold mine, which were interlaced on the table. "I just want to say that I'm here for you, okay?"

"Damn," I mumble.

"What?"

"Those two have really raised a fantastic girl." I smile. "You'll be the best doctor this country has ever seen."

"If I get in."

"You will," I say with conviction. I'm not trying to give her false hope or trying to reward her for the way she's handling this new piece of information. I just happen to feel from the bottom of my heart that this is the inescapable truth.

"Ian?" I look up when I hear someone calling my name.

It's the boy I met at the mall, who gave me his phone number. His hazel eyes seem tired, but his smile widens when he recognizes me, and the eyes get scrunched into two thin lines on his face. His teeth are a little crooked and yellow but so very cute. What's his name again?

"Gustavo!" I say, suddenly remembering it. My hands are shiny from the burger grease, so I hand him my arm to shake. "Did you take your test here, too?"

"Hey, you were in my classroom, weren't you?" Vanessa asks, looking at him.

"Two thirteen? Wait a second, you're the girl who borrowed my extra pen, right?"

"What?" I ask, my eyes wide. "Vanessa, you didn't bring extra pens?"

"I, actually, I . . . kinda forgot to bring my pencil case, what with changing backpacks and everything, so I didn't have a single pen," she answers, embarrassed. Then she looks at Gustavo and, narrowing her eyes, adds, "And Ian didn't have to know about this!"

"Oh, God, I'm so sorry! Is he your boyfriend?"

"Ew!" Vanessa gasps, and Gustavo laughs. He obviously knows we're not together. "He's my brother, you perv!"

"He's teasing you, Vanessa," I say, holding back my smile. When did my life become this roller coaster of serious conversations followed by smiles and random people, one after the other? "We met yesterday."

"And he hasn't texted me at all, can you believe it?" he asks Vanessa, crossing his arms. "I'm seriously offended."

"I was . . . busy," I answer, and Vanessa laughs at the situation, finally understanding what's going on.

"I bet you tell everyone that," says Gustavo, sounding dramatic and funny at the same time.

"Busy with Netflix, my friend," Vanessa says, then takes another bite of her sandwich.

This time, Gustavo can't hold back a chuckle. "Okay, that's a losing battle for me." He shrugs. "Well, I need to go home because I'm starving and sleepy, and this line keeps getting longer. It was a pleasure to see you again, Ian."

"I'll text you!" I say when he starts walking away.

"Promises, promises," he says as he leaves.

"Whoa, what was that?" Vanessa asks when Gustavo is out of view. "Why didn't you tell me about him?"

"Because I have no idea what just happened," I answer, astonished.

# CHAPTER 23

# VICTOR

WHEN ERIC AND IAN LEAVE the apartment, silence fills every corner of the living room.

My hand is still on Henrique's head, and his eyes are still closed as he lets me stroke his hair. I feel my heart hammer against my chest, and I'm sure he can hear it under my shirt. The heat emanating from his body makes sweat run down my forehead, but I don't dare move to wipe it off, and I feel two drops trickle down my temple, make their way down my face, and drip onto my shoulder.

The silence between us is peaceful. It's one of those times when you don't want to say anything for fear of ruining a magical moment, but I still feel as if I should say something. My mom likes to say that whenever silence takes over a room, it's because an angel is passing by and drawing all the attention. I'll have to be the one to send the angel packing.

"I have to apologize," I say in a murmur, taking my hand off Henrique's hair and wiping the sweat from my forehead.

I take a deep breath, feeling my heart beat out of control. He opens his eyes.

And that's it. The sound of reality finally seeps into this nice moment between us, my words destroying the peace created by the angel that just flew out the window.

Henrique shuffles his body forward and then turns to face me, his back propped against the pillows around the left arm of the couch. I look at him, and we watch each other like two human beings who've just discovered they're not alone in the world, delighted by each other's existence.

"I'm not sure how to make you believe me, Henrique, but this is the truth: I am so sorry. I'm sorry for everything I said and for the words I used, because I know they were cruel and false." I can feel my eyes tearing up, my nostrils dilating, and my palms getting even sweatier. "My God, I like you so much, and I really wish that what we have can last! And I know I threw it all away when I said those things, but now I realize how unfair they were. I can't imagine what you must be thinking with all of this, but I want you to know that I am here for whatever you need. Even if we don't work out and nothing else ever happens between the two of us, I need you to know that I don't want to disappear from your life—that I want to help you whenever I can, because you're way too good to face this awful world alone."

I look away, then stare at the floor, because I don't know what else to say and I'm already starting to repeat myself, and my head is beginning to spin.

Then I feel the cold tips of his fingers on my chin when he lifts my face to make me look him in the eye.

"I need to apologize, too. I was too headstrong," he says, and my body seems to relax immediately. I wipe the tears on my face and smile, feeling a mix of joy and relief. "I also said cruel things and retreated into my shell, because that's how I deal with life. Maybe I have this idea that things should always be under my control, but that's not how it works. We're the sum of different feelings in this world full of prejudice and bad people. And I know I was a jerk when I thought you'd be nothing but another disappointment, because maybe I already wanted to be disappointed and just needed an excuse to say that I was much better than all the other people in this world. But you made me see that there's also beauty in all the chaos, Victor, and for that, I'll be forever grateful."

His eyes travel all over my face, looking at the blue streak in my hair,

and my eyebrows,

and the scars from my pimples,

and the few beard hairs on my cheeks,

and my eyes,

and my nose,

and my lips.

I smile and he smiles, and I see his face coming closer, and I feel the warmth of his body become more intense with every second, like a star that just exploded and has found its rightful place in the universe.

When our lips touch, it's not a fierce kiss, but the type of kiss that seems to seal a deal. And yet, my heartbeat is out of step, my body is electrified, and the hair on the back of my neck is up.

His head moves away after a few seconds and he hugs me, and this time I'm the one burying my face in his shoulder. Now he's the one protecting me.

"You are so important to me," I mutter, my mouth muffled by the fabric of his T-shirt. "Thank you for being in my life."

"You are the most fascinating person I've ever met," he answers, letting go of me and grinning. "Thank *you* for being in my life."

Now he's the one smiling, and I'm the one aiming for his lips. And this time it's a passionate kiss, as if his lips were my source of oxygen.

He lies on the couch, and before I know it I'm already on top of him, kissing him with a carnal desire, a long movie kiss, wanting to take all the good things he has to offer and to repay him with everything I can give. We connect with each other through our lips, our interlaced fingers, the heat of our bodies, and the coordinated rhythm of our breaths, cutting the silence of a thousand angels passing through the room.

"Do you have a condom?" I whisper in his ear.

Henrique stands up from the couch and takes my hand. "I do," he says, and leads me to his room.

The rest is pure symphony.

+

Sandra arrives before Eric or Ian, and she isn't sure how to react when she finds the two of us alone in the apartment, our hair wet from the shower, my white cheeks rosy from the heat. I had called her as soon as we decided Carlos couldn't get away with this without any consequences.

"You sorted things out?" she asks, looking from me to Henrique. "You sorted things out!"

Then she hugs us, and Henrique seems a little awkward, but there's nothing he can do about it. She covers us in kisses and only then seems to remember there's a reason she's here.

"My God, I'm so insensitive! Is everything all right with you, Henrique?"

"Now it is," he answers, smiling.

"That's kind of the reason we called you," I add, and Sandra raises an eyebrow. "The more help, the better."

Then I tell her more or less what we are planning on doing later.

"You're evil geniuses. I love it," Sandra says.

"It's all Eric's fault. It was his idea," I tell her.

"Are we really going to do it?" Henrique asks. He still seems uncertain about the whole thing, and even though I get it, I don't let him back away.

"Tonight," I answer. As fate would have it, the front door flies open as Eric and three more boys loaded with clothes, makeup, and a string of playful insults enter the apartment like a hurricane.

Everyone hugs and kisses us, offering Henrique solidarity, asking if everything is fine with him, how he's dealing with the whole situation, and if he needs anything. From what Henrique told me, none of Eric's friends knew about his status, but none of them seem to treat him differently or mind it at all.

The dining room table is soon covered in clothes, and the sound of everyone changing into their drag personas takes over the room. Sandra watches in astonishment as the boys put glue on their eyebrows and start applying their makeup with professional mastery, and she works up the courage to ask one of them to do her makeup for tonight. They all start fighting over who's going to do her makeup, and Sandra feels like the most important person in the room.

Ian arrives a little later, already wearing some old outfit, a backpack with a change of clothes, and a wonderful scent of cologne. He attracts the girls' attention with his arms exposed in a sleeveless shirt and a pair of tight jean shorts that look like they haven't been worn in a few years. He smiles when the comments start, but he doesn't pay much attention, focusing instead on the details of what we're about to do.

"You realize the police might arrive at any moment, right?" Ian asks, crouched next to Eric, helping him with the balloons, careful not to pop them and make the living room an even bigger mess. Ian and Eric delicately separate the balloons into different bags, and when they're done, Eric gets a towel for Ian to clean his hands so he can get changed into something more presentable.

"Then we just run," Eric informs us after he washes his hands, sitting on a free chair in front of the mirror and starting a complex makeup procedure.

"In those heels?" Sandra looks at the girls' shoes, scattered all over the floor, and none of them is shorter than four inches. Nicolle Lopez grabs Sandra's chin and pulls it up, telling her to close her eyes so she can finish the Amy Winehouse look.

"We practice every weekend, running away from assholes downtown, my dear," Mad Madonna says, zipping up her red thigh-high boots, *Kinky Boots*–style, and arranges her blond wig to make it look as real as possible. "Don't you go around thinking anyone can catch us that easy."

Sandra thinks about saying something back, but when she sees Mad Madonna get up so easily, she realizes they know what they're talking about.

"There you go!" Nicolle says, giving Sandra a pat on the shoulder.

Sandra opens her eyes and looks at herself in the mirror, astounded. Her eyes seem bigger from the eyeliner, and her eyelids are covered in a green shadow that make her look like Poison Ivy.

"You are *really* great at this!" Sandra pulls out her phone and starts taking dozens of selfies. "One of these is definitely going to be my new profile pic."

Eric, now transformed into Bibi Montenegro with a violet leotard, an Afro wig with the tips dyed blond, and makeup that highlights her black skin, claps and calls everyone's attention. "Ladies! Is everyone ready?"

"Take it easy, Bibi!" Kara Parker yells, still in the process of gluing on her blue eyelash extensions.

"Speed it up, dammit!" Bibi says, then looks around and smiles.

"First of all, thanks to all the girls who canceled their plans at the last minute to stick up for our friend Henrique. This guy is my little brother, maybe even the most important person in my life, and to see what happened to him, to feel my blood boil, it just made me more certain that I've loved him since the day we first started this crazy friendship."

I see Henrique's eyes are shimmering with Eric's sudden display of affection.

"You know what this calls for?" Henrique gets off the couch suddenly and runs to the kitchen. In less than a minute, he comes back with a bunch of plastic cups in one hand and a half-full gallon of wine in the other.

"The two of you have a bizarre tradition of toasting important moments with horrible drinks," Kara Parker mumbles, taking a cup from Henrique's hand. "Come on, pour it before I regret it!"

Henrique passes out the cheap wine, and Bibi raises her glass.

"A toast to Henrique!" she shouts.

"To Henrique!" they all echo in unison, downing the wine.

It's official: Operation Rainbow is a go.

# CHAPTER 24

# HENRIQUE

WE CALL THE TAXI COMPANY that always drives us to the nightclubs, and they seem surprised when we order three cars. The operator asks if she heard right, and when I say yes, the only reason she doesn't hang up on me is because I'm a regular, so she knows it's not a prank.

The cars arrive in less than ten minutes, parking in single file in front of our building. We're already waiting downstairs, drawing attention from every passerby: four drag queens with rainbow-colored clothes, three boys, and a girl carrying plastic bags full of heavy balloons that are firmly tied up so they won't burst, as well as a speaker big enough that it takes as much space as another passenger.

The taxis form a caravan to a quiet and peaceful street in Copacabana that still has some houses that haven't been replaced by skyscrapers. Trees ornament both sides of the street, and the lampposts provide plenty of light. *Perfect. The more people who can see us, the better.*

It's almost eleven o'clock at night and there isn't a lot of activity here, but some people still stare in curiosity when the taxis pull up in the quiet neighborhood and all these people in every color of the rainbow get out. We ask the drivers to leave because we don't want them to end up in trouble in case anything goes wrong. But after hearing what we're about to do and why, the three drivers refuse to leave and say they'll wait for us on the next block and that if anything happens we should just run and they'll be there. They've all driven us plenty of times over the years, and they know we're not vandals but protesters.

As people walk by and turn their heads to check us out, we get organized.

"Where's his place?" Bibi asks, looking around.

I point to the left of the street and we all cross, facing the pristine wall surrounding Carlos's house. An electrified barrier tops the concrete wall, and there are no signs of graffiti or even a line drawn by a kid passing by on his way home from school. Sandra crouches down to untie the bags and, as if she were handling grenades, passes the paint-filled balloons to each of the ladies.

"Who wants to go first?" Sandra asks.

Bibi positions herself and gestures to Victor, who hits play on the speaker. It has enough battery to keep playing for at least an hour, and the first mad guitar chords of the Cazuza song "O Tempo Não Para" start booming.

And when the lights in the houses around us start turning on and curious heads appear at the windows, Bibi throws the first balloon at the wall around Carlos's house, and it explodes in an intense shade of green that sprinkles all over the concrete.

Everyone claps and shouts, calling even more attention to ourselves.

While Cazuza sings that he's shooting against the sun, that he's strong and haphazard, Mad Madonna throws a balloon that explodes in a shade of violet; when he sings that he's tired of running in the opposite direction without a podium finish or the kiss of a girlfriend, Kara Parker throws a balloon that bursts orange; when he sings that the dice are still being cast because time doesn't stop, Nicolle Lopez throws a balloon that explodes in yellow; when he sings that every other day he survives without a scratch, Ian is the one who grabs a balloon and throws it, and it explodes in blue; when the pool is full of rats and the ideas don't correspond to facts, Victor grabs the second to last and throws it, and it explodes in indigo; and when, at last, Cazuza sings that he keeps seeing the future repeating the past and that he sees a museum full of novelties, I throw the last balloon, which explodes in a shade of red.

Time doesn't stop, and everyone is yelling at us from their windows, wondering what's going on, telling us to turn off the music. We see the lights in the house behind the wall turn on.

"Would you like to do the honors before we run away?" Bibi asks, handing me a can of black spray paint. I take the can and shake it, feeling the ink mix inside the container.

I've never spray-painted anything before, but it's easy. The black ink that comes out doesn't mix with the paint that's running down the wall in an explosion of colors.

I write out the words, and we scramble to take a photo. I ask Sandra, Victor, and Ian not to be in it, because the photo will go online and I don't know how that would affect their lives, and unwillingly the three of them agree. Thanks to Victor's background in film and the camera that Eric got from one of the photographers who covers nightlife in Rio, all we need is one click to get the perfect shot: All four drag queens, wearing the colors of the rainbow, and me, in a white T-shirt with a red ribbon, smiling by the words I spray-painted on the wall:

# HIV DOESN'T KILL
# PREJUDICE DOES

+

**Henrique Andrade** shared a photo
2 HOURS AGO

So, as you can see in the photo above, this happened: A few friends and I decided to take matters into our own graffiti hands and solve a little issue that happened to me this past week. Let me explain. Maybe you know, or maybe you don't, but the owner of this wall exposed my HIV-positive status online without my permission, which is not only a crime but also shows the character of someone who thinks he has the power to make me "regret" not bending to his wishes. His post went viral, and I received thousands of comments, both positive and negative, from well-intentioned people and from some who think they can point a finger and judge others without even knowing them. And that judgment even manifested as graffiti right outside my house, with words that weren't exactly as positive or colorful as mine.

I've decided to pay him back in kind, and the result is the explosion of color you see here.

Here's what I need to tell the owner of the wall in this picture: I am fine, Carlos. For real. I have absolutely no regrets—not even for the time I said I didn't want anything to do with you anymore, ever since the day you decided to disappear. As you've already noticed, all our actions have consequences, and I wish all of them could be as beautiful as the unity represented in this photo, or as colorful as the people who take me in day after day and love me no matter what happens. The consequence of your actions, to me, was that I realized there's a network of people who love me as I am, who don't judge me for my past, and who teach me, every day, to discover how beautiful and full of color my life can be.

I hope these colors will help you to see how different human beings can be—that not all of them are cruel or willing to make you feel bad just for being who you are. There was a time when I felt bad, when I tried to blame other people, and when I questioned, daily, what had caused my life to take the course it did. But I learned, Carlos—in the passing days, and months, and years—that my life is far too important to be wasted with negative feelings, with ideas that only bring me down instead of up, with thoughts that only get in the way and are of no help. So I decided, way back when you disappeared from my life, that it wasn't worth it, to suffer for inevitable things and that, instead, I had to focus on being the best version of myself. Today I understand that you were essential to that process.

And for that, I thank you.

3,658 likes
2,200 comments

# EPILOGUE

# IAN

*Six months later*

GABRIEL AND DANIELA'S WEDDING IS beautiful. It was officiated by a five-foot-tall woman with a powerful voice that hypnotized everyone. It's silly, but at first I was nervous to be chosen as Gabriel's best man. But now the sweat running down my temples isn't from nervousness but from all the activity in the venue, where everyone's eating and drinking. I'm squeezed into a tux, and my parents are acting like two children, taking photos with their phones as if I were the one getting married. I pass around a tray with the groom's tie to collect funds for their honeymoon (a very Brazilian wedding tradition), cutting off pieces of the tie and handing one to everyone who contributes. Toward the back, the

DJ gets everyone dancing, and all the women are either in flip-flops or barefoot, tossing aside their high heels and perfect posture from the reception.

I've never been as happy for two people as I am now. Gabriel is overjoyed, and I'm sure he made the world's best impulsive decision when he asked Daniela to marry him. He's already taken off his suit jacket, wearing only a button-down shirt, and the sleeves are rolled up and half the buttons are undone. He's totally drunk, dancing next to his wife.

Vanessa is also glowing, as she has been ever since she learned that she got into medical school. The only thing worrying her is that she'll need to move to another city, and she wakes up in the middle of the night to make notes of items that she can't forget to pack. Mom and Dad are proud and sad at the same time, but I'll stay home for a few more years and make sure that their transition to empty nesters won't be too painful for them.

Ever since Henrique wrote the post, his story has taken a monumental turn. At first, it ended up in local online newspapers, and it all exploded from there. The story was picked up by newspapers (both national and international) and TV shows, and suddenly everyone was talking about it—teachers, YouTubers, film and TV producers, LGBTQ+ and HIV activists. Everyone wants a piece of him and his drag queen friends, who are now known as the Fabulous Four. They even did a series of ten performances around clubs in Rio de Janeiro before—just like every single pop group—they started fighting and broke up. Henrique proved Andy Warhol's words true by getting his fifteen minutes of fame, but the dust settled as suddenly as it went up, and his life soon returned to normal.

From what we've heard, Carlos's parents were furious with Henrique and threatened to sue him, but when they learned that exposing someone's HIV status publicly was a much more serious crime than vandalism—and what lovely, colorful vandalism it was!—the threats stopped and they just let it go. We learned that Carlos had gone back to New Zealand, though whether or not he did so willingly remains a mystery.

Gosh, what else has happened since then? Oh, yeah—I'm undetectable! It happened much more quickly than I imagined it would, and now my doctor's appointments are every four months, just to make sure everything is okay. My doctor is more concerned about a small rise in my triglyceride levels than with the HIV, which to me means I have absolutely nothing to complain about, except for the sacrifice of having to avoid fried food.

"HERE'S FIFTY BUCKS!" I hear a voice yelling from behind me, and I turn around, holding Gabriel's tie in shambles.

"OPA!" Gustavo smiles and throws the bill on the tray, grabbing his piece of the tie.

You didn't think I'd forgotten about him, did you? We're still getting to know each other, but things have been great between us. He got into the economics program, and now he comes to my house every month and kidnaps all my Hal Varian textbooks. My parents didn't want him there at first, but time worked its magic, and he's now sitting by my side at the table Gabriel picked for my family, holding my hand. Still not the ideal, but if my mom or dad minds, at least they don't make the situation uncomfortable.

I still haven't told them about the HIV, and I know that, when the day comes, it will be a difficult conversation. I want to be ready for their reaction, but what I can say is that today I'm still not ready. Even if the people around me are the best support system a person could ask for, my parents' opinions are still so important to me. And I know, deep inside, that their love is bigger than any bad news I could give them.

I look away from my parents and catch Gustavo's smile. I smile back.

And, in this moment, I'm reminded of when we were alone for the first time. Of the oppressive silence in his bedroom. Of the thoughts swirling in my head: *He's going to kick me out when I tell him, he'll say things will never work out between us, that he doesn't want this, tell me to get away, block me from all forms of contact, and everything we've built will be completely destroyed because of this virus.* I remember the posters that hung on his wall, kept there as a reminder of his younger teenage years—Paramore, Evanescence, Fall Out Boy, and My Chemical Romance; I think back to the mess on his desk, with fantasy novels scattered everywhere, none of them read because he said he'd bought them when he decided he liked fantasy, even though he'd never read a single book in the genre; pieces of paper with scribbled compositions, paired with books on music theory; a guitar behind the door that has never made it out of its leather case, from when he decided he'd be a musician; an umbrella that looked as if it'd been stolen from Mary Poppins, which he's also never used because he's weird and prefers to walk in the rain.

I remember him kissing me, and that his body was warm, but I was hyperventilating.

"Are you nervous?" he asked.

"I am."

"You don't have to be."

"I have to tell you something." Then I backed away from him, got up from the bed, and sat down on his desk chair. "I'm HIV-positive."

He blinked, once, twice, three times, processing the information.

"I have condoms," he said with such simplicity that it scared me.

This time *I* blinked once, twice, three times, processing the information.

"You're not running away? You're not done with me?"

"I like you, Ian. And I have condoms. Multiple."

So I smiled, and he smiled back, and it was never a problem again. He only asked if he could come to an appointment at the clinic, where he asked the doctor more questions than a mother with a new-born child who just got their first fever. He even got started on PrEP just to make sure he's extra-protected against contracting HIV.

We only talk about HIV when I want to talk about it or when he has a question.

And we've been together ever since.

And I've been happy ever since.

I am not alone.

Everything is all right.

# AUTHOR'S NOTE

The idea to write *Where We Go From Here* came to me when I was working as a technical reviewer for a health periodical at the Oswaldo Cruz Foundation, an important government organization that, among other things, produces and distributes free antiretroviral medication for HIV in Brazil. My job basically required me to revise library references, but every once in a while, I found myself reading articles that piqued my interest. One of the articles I read talked about the perception Brazilians have of HIV, as well as the social impacts of those beliefs. What I read in these articles— that people believe HIV is a punishment from God, that it's a virus that affects only the gay community, that one could contract the virus through saliva or sweat, and other misconceptions—made me realize that we haven't come quite as far as we'd like to believe when it comes to social stigmas against HIV-positive people, whether in Brazil or around the world.

Writing this book was a process that demanded great effort, because while I wanted to write a story that could be important for other people, I also needed to confront my own understanding of what it's like to be an HIV-positive person in the twenty-first century. I was twenty-three years old, working eight hours a day, and finishing my master's thesis. It wasn't a particularly tranquil time in my life.

So I started researching: How is HIV treatment offered by the Sistema Único de Saúde (Single Health System) in Brazil? What are the psychological and social implications affecting HIV-positive people? In addition to educating myself about these facts, I also sought the advice of doctors and patients at treatment centers that I visited. After everything I read and heard, I decided to turn what I learned into a fictional story that is linear and coherent, and the best way I found to do that was to create three characters who deal with HIV in distinct ways.

Ian, Victor, and Henrique are at different stages of life when the story begins, and these three points of view were vital in bringing attention to the nuances of HIV and the idea that life can continue to be wonderful with or without it. My intention was always to make sure the story was good-humored and could convey a welcoming message, even if the characters weren't always at their best. So I made a point of creating a world very similar to my own, where we count on our families, whether they are families by blood or ones we chose.

The characters' journeys to acceptance and self-acceptance needed to culminate in a message that would bring hope to the reader. For this reason, I chose to end the story with a song by Cazuza. Perhaps you're not familiar with him, but during the 1980s, Cazuza was an important singer in the Brazilian music scene; today, everyone in my country knows at least one of his songs. He was also openly bisexual and one of the first Brazilian public figures to discuss his HIV-positive status during the AIDS crisis. From one of his last and most powerful presentations came the song "O Tempo Não Para" ("Time Doesn't Stop")—referenced at the end of this novel—where the singer, already debilitated by the advancement of the disease, sings about how one must continue to move forward, knowing that life must be lived to its fullest, because life is cruel and doesn't stop for even one second.

This song is of great importance not just to me but to the larger context of discussions surrounding HIV and AIDS in Brazil, and I knew it would fit in perfectly at the end of this story. The edition you hold in your hands has been translated for an audience that likely doesn't know who Cazuza was, and perhaps the song doesn't carry as much weight for that reason, but know that it is important and even today resonates as one of the greatest songs by an artist who shined a light on the topic of HIV at a time when not speaking about the problem was the easiest way to deal with it.

And therein lie the goals of this book: It seeks to discuss a topic that is still conditioned by silence; to question prejudices that surround us; to help us reflect on the motives that lead us to have them; and, above all, to promote empathy and demonstrate that life is beautiful, just like a wall covered in colorful paint.

Lucas Rocha
May 2019

# AFTERWORD

In 1981, a strange health affliction began affecting gay men in the United States' largest cities, including Los Angeles, San Francisco, and New York. Many people were dying quickly, and no one knew why. When scientists first discovered it was a disease that could destroy the body's immune system, there was nothing they could do about it. There were no medications, no one knew how to prevent it, and it was spreading throughout the world. The following year, in 1982, the Centers for Disease Control and Prevention (CDC) gave this affliction a name—acquired immune deficiency syndrome (AIDS)—but it took until 1984 for researchers to discover the virus that causes AIDS. That virus would officially be called human immunodeficiency virus (HIV) in 1986, and it has been known as that ever since.

As researchers learned more about HIV and AIDS, new medications were developed to treat HIV-positive people. By the mid-1990s, an "AIDS cocktail" was made available, which dramatically extended the life expectancy of people living with HIV. Since then, medications have continued to improve, and today HIV-positive people who follow proper treatment can live long and healthy lives with as little as one pill a day. Moreover, we know that HIV-positive people who follow treatment and have achieved an undetectable viral load cannot transmit the virus to others, otherwise known as undetectable = untransmittable, or U = U.

Additionally, detection methods have greatly improved over the years. In many places in the UK, people can walk into medical facilities and get screened for HIV in just a few minutes, receiving same-day results. There are also new medications, like pre- and post-exposure prophylaxis (PrEP and PEP, respectively), that can be taken by HIV-negative people to prevent them from contracting HIV, in addition to condom use. Getting tested regularly and, if diagnosed with HIV, beginning treatment as soon as possible are currently the best ways to prevent transmission and improve population health.

But while researchers have made great strides in detecting and treating HIV since the 1980s, access to testing and treatment varies worldwide. In *Where We Go From Here*, we meet three young men in Rio de Janeiro, Brazil, whose lives are affected by HIV to varying extents. And while the experiences of Ian, Victor, and Henrique provide a glimpse of what it might be like to live with HIV in Brazil today, it is important to understand that HIV treatment in Brazil differs in some ways from treatment in the UK.

In Brazil, HIV treatment is fully funded through the nation's Sistema Único de Saúde (Single Health System). Whereas, in the UK, the NHS provides free HIV treatment to residents, regardless of immigration status. Over the page are contact details of various organisations which can help and support people affected by HIV. Whatever your circumstances might be, know that there are resources out there for you.

# Helpline Information

If you or anyone close to you has been affected by any of the issues in *Where We Go From Here*, here are some organisations in the UK that offer help, advice and support. Ian realises he is not alone, and neither are you.

**National Heath Service** • nhs.uk/conditions/hiv-and-aids • 111
Overview of HIV and AIDs, with links to treatment and support information.

**Terrence Higgins Trust** • tht.org.uk • 0808 802 1221
Free and confidential services for people with HIV and AIDS, including advice and representation on welfare rights, housing and legal matters, practical advice and befriending.

**Positively UK** • positivelyuk.org • 0207 7713 044 • info@positivelyuk.org
Support for the emotional and physical wellbeing of people with HIV, including advice on treatment, talking about HIV with others, relationships and employment options. Most staff and volunteers are living with HIV so have first-hand experience of the condition.

**National AIDS Trust** • nat.org.uk • 0207 8146 767 • info@nat.org.uk
The UK's leading charity dedicated to campaigning for change in society's response to HIV. They provide expert advice and practical resources.

**Body and Soul Charity** • bodyandsoulcharity.org • 0207 9236 880 • enquiries@bodyandsoulcharity.org
A UK charity dedicated to transforming the lives of children, teenagers and families living with, or affected by, HIV.

**NAM Aidsmap** • aidsmap.com • 0203 7270 123 • info@nam.org.uk
Information, news and resources for people with HIV and AIDS, comprehensive information on treatment and a database of HIV clinics in the UK.

**Free HIV Testing** • freetesting.hiv • 0203 9811 772 • sh24.info@nhs.net
Free self-sampling HIV tests are available for residents in some areas in England.

# ACKNOWLEDGMENTS

Writing a book might be a solitary task, but after it's finished comes a list of incredible people. And there have been plenty of those over the months in which *Where We Go From Here* was read, reread, revised, cut, and polished to arrive in your hands in its current form.

This is the moment to remember each person who has been with me along this small journey.

First of all, my three pillars: Suely, Rodolfo, and Diego (aka my mom, dad, and brother, respectively). You are the best family a person could ask for, and I feel profoundly lucky to have you by my side. Thank you for all the support and for always being present in my life. I love you all.

To my agent, Gui Liaga, from Página 7 Agency, who gave me all the support I needed to turn this book into a reality. Without her, you would probably have nothing but promises of a story that would never have been finished. Thank you for adding so much to this plot and for getting it out of my drawer. You're an amazing woman!

A special thanks to Galera Record and to my editor, Ana Lima, as well as the whole team who made this book even better. I am so lucky that I got to publish my first story with a publishing house I admire so much and that makes a difference in so many people's lives. Definitely the best choice I could've made.

To my little group of writers, proofreaders, agents, and people involved in this delightful world of books: Bárbara Morais, Taissa Reis, Dayse Dantas, Fernanda Nia, Babi Dewet, Felipe Castilho, Valéria Alves, Pam Gonçalves, Vitor Martins, and Vitor Castrillo. You are my daily support for venting, complaining, and celebrating, and my life wouldn't be as wonderful if you weren't in it.

To the people in the US who have turned this book into a reality for North American readers: First of all, to David Levithan, the person responsible for carrying the Brazilian edition across a hemisphere and bringing it to Scholastic; to my US editor, Orlando Dos Reis, for championing this story, and for his advice on what would sound better in this version; to Larissa Helena, my English translator, for understanding my dorky jokes and making them as funny (or as unfunny) as they are in Brazilian Portuguese; to Josh Berlowitz, Kerianne Steinberg, and all the Scholastic team who worked so hard and were so energetic about this book from the start. You are amazing!

To the friends who inspire me every single day and who helped me, directly or indirectly, while I wrote this story: Thales Souza, Lucas Figueiredo, Marcelle Almeida, Mariana Saadi, and Ariadne Pacheco, for following the same academic path as me and for hearing about this story on Thursdays; Luiza Nunes, the first to hear about the outlines for this idea, on a stone bench at Fiocruz, for being excited about something still so loose; Jéssyca Santiago and Mariana Moraes, who were perhaps more excited about the release of this book than anyone else; Fábio Laranjeira and Jean Amaral, two essential people whom I am fortunate to call my friends; and finally, Ana Cristina Rodrigues—not a day goes by when I don't feel thankful that you came into my life. If it weren't for you, I'd hardly be the writer I am today—I'd hardly be a writer, to be completely honest.

To everyone who was willing to talk to me and teach me so much when I went to the clinics during the first drafts of this book: not just the doctors, who helped me with the more technical parts of this book (thank you, Dr. Ana and Dr. Marcelo!), but especially to the patients receiving treatment and the people waiting for their test results in the rapid testing line. I remember some of your names, and others are just images in my mind, but know that, without you, this book wouldn't have come to life. Thank you for the support, for the smiles, and the will to keep living that each of you displayed. If inspiration could take a form, I'd want it to be the expressions I saw on the faces of every person when they told me life must be lived to the fullest.

And, finally, to the most important person in this entire process: you, the reader. I hope Ian's, Victor's, and Henrique's lives might make some kind of difference, that you may have learned something new, or at least smiled and understood that as hard as the journey can seem at first, at some point, it becomes peaceful and full of amazing moments. And we have our whole lives ahead of us!

# ABOUT THE AUTHOR

Lucas Rocha is a librarian from Rio de Janeiro but lives in São Paulo. He splits his time between writing and working at a public library, where he works with children, teens, and adults of all different backgrounds. *Where We Go From Here*, an LGBTQ+ novel about the importance of friendship and found families, is his first novel.